MEMORIES ARE MADE

A Romantic Thriller

by Fred Pascoe

CONTENTS

ACKNOWLEDGMENTS

To my darling wife, Sylvia who has remained loyal and supportive through all our trials and tribulations. One of life's big mysteries. And I do promise to catch up with all those outstanding jobs I've left while writing this novel.

Also to Stuart Alexander, friend and neighbour, who kindly edited the draft manuscript and corrected innumerable errors. Much appreciated and many thanks. Any errors found are mine alone when adding additional material to the original work.

Fred Pascoe

FOREWORD

The Snake Pass or Snake Road is on the A57, which runs through the Peak District between Sheffield and Manchester. It winds and twists as it climbs over the back of the Pennines. In summer tourists flock to the Peak District in their thousands to admire, photograph and enjoy the raw beauty of the Pennines, also known as the Backbone of England. But come winter it is not for the faint hearted. The area in winter is notorious for heavy snow falls and blizzards causing drifts that can hide a high-sided lorry. The Snake Pass (named not because of the twists and sharp bends but after the Snake Inn) is often closed in winter by bad weather and also by subsidence after heavy rain.

The Snake is overlooked by another famous landmark - Kinder Scout, also known as the Dark Peak, and is a gritstone plateau with deep cloughs cut into the peat. It is a place to avoid after dark unless you are an experienced hiker, dressed in the right outdoor clothes and with good emergency equipment. There are occasions when weather conditions produce a whiteout, a white fog so dense a hiker cannot see more than a foot or two ahead. And having personally experienced one when trying to find a way off Kinder, it is remembered as the most frightening of the many hikes across the Dark Peak.

PROLOGUE

A mist was forming on the Snake Pass as the Mercedes saloon descended the steep hill. Headlights blazing, speed increasing by the second, it aimed at the temporary warning barrier guarding a recent land slip. The KIA SUV travelling behind urged it on. It crashed through the barrier as the man inside opened the driver's door and hauled himself halfway out. The car took a flying leap into the ravine and he clung to the door, confused and disoriented as it smashed nose down onto the rocky hillside. The force of the car hitting the ground loosened his grip and the speed of it summersaulting onto its roof threw him like a sling shot away from the car and dumped him in a heather filled hollow.

The car slid further down the hillside on its roof until it was stopped by a large rock. Flames from petrol leaking onto a hot exhaust manifold emerged from the bonnet, lighting up the darkness and pushing against the mist. Blue flames raced along the body of the car, riding a trail of petrol and blew the petrol tank. The explosion shot a massive fireball skywards, the fierce heat sizzling mist into steam.

Two hikers, one of them hobbling badly and using a pair of trekking poles to take his weight off his injured ankle, came round the top bend just as the explosion rattled their ears and the fireball lit up the pass below them.

They stopped in awe. The man with the injured ankle leaned heavily on the poles. "Christ, Dave! What the hell was that?"

"That was a petrol tank exploding. God help if there was anyone in the vehicle. Come on, Mick."

"Go, man! You know I'll not keep up."

Dave hesitated, torn between staying with his injured mate or rushing to the crash site.

"Go! I'll follow you down." Mick raised one pole as if to give his mate a dig. "And I'll ring the emergency services from up here. Better chance of a reception."

Dave set off at a run, his rainproof clothes restricting his movements. He was halfway down to the crash site when he saw the rear lights of a car go on and pull away from a shadowed area just beyond the damaged barrier. Well, blow me, he thought. It would have been a right bastard to drive away without seeing if help was needed. By the time he reached the crash site he was gasping for breath and soaked in sweat, his waterproofs locking in his body heat He pulled off his bobble hat and stuffed it in his pocket. Unzipping his jacket he looked down to where the car was still burning. The flames and black acrid smoke swirled around the wreck, and several small fires from the explosion were scattered around the gully, the wet heather damping them down. The flickering flames danced black shadows over the rocks and into the hollows.

He knew without doubt no one could have survived that inferno.

The ravine wasn't deep but the land-slip had created a sheer drop where the car had gone over. He switched on the torch he'd been carrying, shining the beam around the crash site.. He saw a splash of white, partly hidden by the rocks He steadied the beam and strained his eyes... it looked like a white shirt and part of a white face. "Bloody heck!" He moved the torchlight around the immediate hillside, searching for a way down. There.... a place where it was less steep with a sheep trail leading down into the gully. He walked the short distance back up the hill to get to it and was about to climb over a low wall when he heard Mick's trekking poles hitting the road and saw his dim outline hobbling down the hill. He waited.

"Got through," Mick said as he approached. "Ambulance be here in fifteen, twenty minutes."

"Good. I'm pretty certain I saw someone down there. Don't know if he's alive. Just on my way to check."

"Do you want me to wait up here for the ambulance?"

"Yes. And could you give Betty a ring for me and tell her we'll probably be much later than we said."

"Yeh, I'll do that. I'll ring Jane as well and explain. Can't see them being very happy with us, though. We're already several hours late."

"Can't be helped, mate," Dave said, before climbing over the wall and picking his way along the narrow trail to where he'd seen the injured person.

The flames from the burning car had died to just a flicker, almost blanked out by the smoke. His torch lit up the hollow and he saw a man wearing the white shirt. The face, the left half that Dave could see, was blood streaked. Blood oozed from a ragged gash just above the temple, staining the blonde hair red. He was unmoving.

Dave used a nearby rock to place his torch so the light shone on the man. Then he knelt down to take hold of a wrist and feel for a pulse. It was several seconds before he found the faint irregular throb beneath the cold skin, making Dave wonder if the heart was about to stop. He wished he had more medical knowledge. He noticed the shirt had become wet and transparent in the damp chill air, showing there were no under garments. Dave took off his own waterproof jacket and draped it over the man, he knew it was important to keep him warm. Then he remembered his emergency medical kit, opened a side pocket of his backpack and took out a plastic bag containing assorted plasters, a couple of crepe bandages and a medicated lint dressing. Trying not to move the man too much, he gently lifted the head, placed the dressing over the wound and awkwardly wrapped the bandage around the head as best he could. He used a plaster to fasten the bandage.

Mick shouted from the road above, shining his torch to pick out Dave. "What's happening down there?"

"Man seriously injured. Just give me a minute, Mick."

"Do you want me to try and get down to help?"

"Don't be so bloody daft, man. Stay where you are."

"All right! No need to get your knickers in a twist."

Dave didn't bother to answer. He ran his eyes over the prone figure, thinking what else he could do. He placed his hand on the man's shoulder. "Stay with us, mate. Help is coming." He immediately felt foolish, knowing the man couldn't hear him. Ah, what the heck, maybe hearing a voice would help. He was bone aching tired. It had been a hard hike over Win Hill, then Loose Hill and up Kinder from Edale. Bloody Kinder, no wonder they called it the Dark Peak. It was on that bleak gritstone plateau Mick had twisted his ankle, so painful he could hardly walk. Give him credit, despite the pain he'd soldiered on. But the constant stops and slow pace shot their finishing time to hell. And they still had to get to Ladybower where they'd parked the car.

A shout from Mick again dragged him out of his increasing depression.

"What?"

Mick was waving his torch beam down the Snake Pass. "I can hear them coming! And I can see their lights."

Dave cocked his head listening and heard the sirens. He couldn't see the lights because he was in the gully. But knowing they were almost here lifted his spirits. He rested his hand lightly on the injured man. "Just hang on, mate. You'll soon be in safe hands." Dave fretted, worrying the man would die before the help he sorely needed would arrive. He watched the road above and eventually saw the strobe lights on several vehicles coming to a halt. He could just make out an ambulance and police car and what looked like a large SUV. Within a few minutes arch lamps stabbed through the darkness and persistent mist, lighting up the area around Dave and the injured man.

Shortly afterward four men, using the same route he had taken, turned up. A burly Police Officer led the way, wearing a high visibility yellow jacket over his uniform and using a police torch. He was followed by two paramedics, also wearing yellow jackets over their uniforms. One of them carried a stretcher, the other a medical bag. A heavy-weight man, dressed in outdoor clothes and carrying a powerful lamp, slouched along at the rear. By the look of the climbing gear draped around him, Dave reckoned he belonged to a mountain rescue team.

"What have we got?" The Police Officer asked, shining his torch on the injured man

"Looks like he got thrown from the car before the tank blew." Dave replied. "His pulse is very weak and he's got a deep cut to his head. He may have some other injuries. But I'm not an expert." He gestured around the hollow. "He was damn lucky to have landed here because he was protected from the explosion and the heather seems to have cushioned his fall."

The Police Officer squinted at the burnt out car. "Have you checked the vehicle?"

"You must be joking." Dave swept an arm towards the smouldering wreck. "Whoever was in there will be burnt to a crisp. And I was more concerned with this poor bugger."

"Right. Well, my colleague will want a statement from you. She's taking one from your mate at the moment. The quicker you give your statement to her the quicker you'll get away."

Dave stared at the Police Officer for several seconds not liking his officious tone.

One of the paramedics had knelt beside the man and started an examination. Now he looked up at Dave. "This your coat?"

"Yes, and I've put that dressing on his head. I wish I could have done more but didn't know what to do for the best." Dave thought he sounded pathetic.

The paramedic handed up the coat. "Hey, don't knock yourself out, pal. You've done good. Keeping him warm and not moving him was the best thing you could have done." While he was speaking he continued his examination. Finally he looked up at the other paramedic who had unwrapped an emergency foil blanket. "Can't see any signs of internal trauma, Phil. He has a few external injuries but they can wait until we get to the wagon." He stood up.

The mountain rescue lad asked, "Do you want the harness rigged, Bill?"

"No." The paramedic said. as he helped his mate wrap the emergency blanket around the man. "We'll use the path. And I want to get him out of here as soon as possible."

"Any identification?" The Police Officer asked.

"Can't say for certain. But I've only patted his pockets. Be able to check better when we get up top."

Dave asked, "Do you think he'll make it?"

"Lap of the Gods, pal. But if you hadn't come along when you did his chances would have been zero."

Dave, feeling he hadn't wasted his time, turned towards the path. The Police Officer started down the hillside heading for the car, but was halted by a shout from the mountain rescue lad. He had been looking over the area by the land slip, and was holding up a bent and twisted front registration plate from the car. The Police Officer backed up and they met a few yards away.

Dave finally started up the path, hoping the poor sod would survive.

PART ONE

CHAPTER 1

10am Monday morning, Clair was in her kitchen, standing at the solid pine table, sifting through the jewellery designs she had created recently. She was wearing a pink silk blouse and loose-fitting black trousers. Her dark wavy hair was pulled back into a pony tail which every so often she brushed unconsciously with her fingers while studying the designs. She loved working at this 200 year pine table, it was just the right height and large enough to allow for the spread of her papers. The kitchen was also her favourite place in the old farm house. It was roomy. having had one of the walls from another room taken away to expand the area when her father and mother owned the property. It faced east and caught the early morning sun, Sometimes the sunrise was so spectacular she stopped what she was doing and just admired the changing colours from red to gold when the clouds were captured by the morning sun.

She expected her sister in a few minutes and hoped to have at least most of the designs ready for her approval. Iris could be very critical, but she had a good eye for costume jewellery and Clair was well aware it was her sister's final judgement that had made a success of her online business. There were now two stacks of designs in front of her. The smaller stack holding those she didn't think would pass Iris's approval. She heard the front door and footsteps along the hall and Iris came into the room, followed by a boyish looking Police Officer, holding his hat in his hand and a serious look on his face. Iris had a grin on her face. "Look who I found standing at your door. I saved him the trouble of finding the bell." She came to a stop and belly laughed at her joke. The bell push was brass vintage and could be seen a hundred yards away. "Wouldn't tell me why he wanted you... I know." Her hazel eyes twinkled. "You've been found out about growing weed in your greenhouse." Iris, turned and gave the Constable a wink.

Clair saw the Officer was not amused. "Not funny, Iris. I'm sorry my sister has a warped sense of humour. What can I do for you?"

"Mrs Birkenshaw?"

'Yes."

"Constable Turner, Mrs Birkenshaw. It's about your husband's car accident Friday evening."

"Oh, my God! Is Ken dead?" Clair's hands flew to her mouth and her eyes opened wide to stare at Turner in horror.

Iris came quickly over to comfort her sister, glaring at Turner the same time. "What the hell do think you're doing? Coming out with shocking news like that?"

Turner's young face turned bright red. "Oh, heck, I'm so sorry. No, he's not dead, but he was seriously injured and taken to Western General. I thought you knew. My sergeant thought the hospital had contacted you by now and I've been sent here to find out more information regarding your husband."

"How bad is he?" Clair said, her voice choked with tears.

Turner's eyes looked sympathetic. "The last I heard he was in a stable condition, Mrs Birkenshaw." He took a deep breath. "I really am sorry for the misunderstanding."

"So you should be," Iris snapped. She had a sudden thought. "Where was it?"

"The accident?"

"Yes, the bloody accident!"

"Snake Pass..." Turner hesitated, choosing his words carefully. "...the car ran off the road and Mr Birkenshaw was apparently thrown from the car before it caught fire."

"Oh! Iris, did you hear what he said? I can't believe it!"

Iris tightened her arms about her sister.

Turner seeing the devastating effect his words had on Clair, tried to clarify what had occurred. "We are just assuming it happened that way, Mrs Birkenshaw. He had no burn marks, you see. But we can't be certain how he came to be where he was found. And there were no witnesses."

Clair unwrapped herself from Iris's arms and took a paper tissue from a box on the table and wiped her eyes and blew her nose. "I must see him."

"I have a telephone number you could ring, Mrs Birkenshaw," Turner said, relieved to do something positive. He pulled a notebook with a pen attached from his jacket pocket and turned some pages until he found the telephone number and used a pen to copy the number onto a blank page, ripped it out and handed it to Clair.

Clair looked at the paper in her hand, gathering her wits together. What was it her father used to say to her; "Face up to life's problems and you'll frighten them away." Not always Dad, not always. She took a deep breath and turned to Iris. "Give Constable Turner a cup coffee or tea or whatever," she said, and left the room. Ten minutes later she was back, noting Turner was standing exactly where she had left him, but looking less crushed and more relaxed. She spoke to Iris who sat at the table, fiddling with the designs and ignoring Turner.

"Like Constable Turner told us, Ken has some serious injuries but is stable and they've moved him out of Intensive Care this morning They also told me I could visit this afternoon. But not before."

Iris stood up. "Do you want me to come with you'"

"No, it's ok. Anyway. you have an hair appointment this afternoon."

"I can cancel, Judy won't mind."

"No need. Ken is in a coma and I just want to see him. Assure myself, really, he's alive and is in good hands. You know what I mean?"

"Of course, love." Iris said, her tone trying to hide her contempt for her sister's husband.

Constable Turner coughed to catch their attention. "Excuse me, Mrs Birkenshaw. But could you just answer a few questions? And then I'll be out of your way."

"Do you have to bother my sister now? Can't you see she's upset!"

"It's ok," Clair said, touching Iris on the arm. "I don't mind and I have some questions of my own." She looked at Turner and gestured for him to follow her from the room.

"Please yourself." Iris muttered to herself,

thinking Clair was far too easy going for her own good.

Clair showed Constable Turner to the garden room where the windows also faced east, and the morning sun was streaming through the french doors. The room, except for a modern settee and three armchairs and a fifty inch TV, was dotted with mismatched antique furniture, a bookcase, crammed with hard cover books, a leather pouffe and a low coffee table. A pendulum wall clock ticked on the wall opposite the door and a large landscape oil painting hung over the wooden mantlepiece. An occasional table held several family photographs. The wooden floor was scattered with a variety of coloured rugs.

Clair motioned Constable Turner to an armchair where he sat, placed his hat on the coffee table, removed his notebook from the breast pocket, and as Clair settled herself in the armchair opposite, he said, "I'd like to apologise again for giving you such a shock, Mrs Birkenshaw."

"Forget it Constable. I understand it wasn't your fault. And I'm wondering why the hospital didn't contact me before you arrived."

"I don't think they are to blame. The delay could have been due to your husband not having any means of identification. We traced him here through the car registration plate."

"But Ken always has his driving licence and credit cards in his back pocket. They are in a small folding wallet."

"Sorry, but nothing like that was found. Maybe it was lost in the fire or fell from his pocket during the accident. I'll query it in my report."

"You said you have no idea how the accident happened?"

Turner shook his head, unconsciously thumbing his notebook while giving her a direct look. "No, and it's something of a mystery, Mrs Birkenshaw. Your husband went through a warning barrier without trying to stop. There were no skid marks, you see, indicating he had not applied the brakes."

"Oh! I find that hard to believe. Ken is a very good driver."

"Well, he had been drinking and there were also signs of drugs. Were you aware he took drugs?"

"Certainly not! Alcohol, yes. Wine and spirits. But when it came to drugs he despised people who took them. Something to do with when he was growing up. He didn't like to talk about it." She paused a moment and decided to be frank. "It is possible Ken had been drinking if he was with friends who liked to go for expensive meals, including wine and spirits. But he would make sure transport was arranged if he knew there would be heavy drinking involved, so he wouldn't have to drive."

Turner raised an eyebrow, scribbled something in his notebook and looked back at Clair. "The accident occurred Friday evening. Weren't you worried when he didn't come home?"

"Ken left home Friday morning for a business meeting in Manchester. He was staying over during the weekend I wasn't expecting him back until this evening."

"Were you in contact with him during this time?"

Such an innocent question. Should she lie? Not something she was very good at, as Ken told her so often. She looked at the fireplace, as if for inspiration. Clair brought her attention back to the Constable. "No, we were not in contact."

"Right," he said, after several seconds had passed. "Mr Birkenshaw is a Property Developer, isn't he?"

"Yes, he is." She was not surprised he knew. Ken was well known in the business world in and around Sheffield and beyond.

"Does he have any business worries?"

"No. Well not as far as I know." Turner's questions was taking her into shark infested waters. "Look, Constable. I will have to get ready for the hospital shortly and I have several things to attend to before I go."

He looked at his watch. "Of course, Mrs Birkenshaw. You have been very helpful." He stuck his book back in his pocket, took his hat off the table and briskly stood up. "I'm sure any other questions can be left for the moment." He strode towards the door.

Clair followed him.

Back in the kitchen, Clair made as if to show him out.

"It's all right, Mrs Birkenshaw, I can find my own way." He nodded pleasantly to both of them before making for the door.

They looked at each other, listening for the front door to close. Except for some facial similarities they did not look like sisters. Clair had dark hair, brown eyes and stood five foot nine in her stocking feet, her slim figure toned with a daily exercise regime. Iris had light brown hair and hazel eyes and at thirty was five years older. She was two inches shorter and nearly a stone heavier, giving her a Monroe figure that attracted the eye of male predators.

"How did it go, love?"

Clair sat down at the table with her sister. "Not too bad. Just a few awkward questions, but nothing serious."

Iris tilted her head. "You going to tell me?"

Clair sighed. "Constable Turner thought it strange we hadn't been in touch with each other. I wasn't about to tell him why. It's just that Ken and I had an awful row on Friday before he left, and I decided I wasn't going to ring him while he was away and he must have thought the same."

"And the row was about?" The hazel in Iris's eyes became tigerish. A look she always had before defending Clair. The look she had when her eleven year old fist slammed into the stomach of the school bully who had been pulling Clair around by her hair.

Clair wished she had kept her mouth shut.

"It was nothing really Just a silly row that got out of hand. You know how it is. Let's just drop it shall we?"

Iris was not convinced, she knew Clair was making light of the row.

Clair, in an effort to change the subject, pulled the stacks of designs toward her. "What do you think?"

Iris's features softened. "They are as good as ever, love. I think you've got some real winners here."

Clair leaned over and gave her sister a hug. "Thanks. But I may not be able to start on them as planned. I'll have to see how Ken is first."

Iris gave Clair a peck on the cheek and stood. "I hope, for your sake he'll be ok." she said, but the cold look in her eyes belied her words.

They said their goodbyes and hugged each other again before Iris left.

CHAPTER 2

It took Clair twenty minutes to drive to Western General, and it took another ten minutes to find a parking place. When she finally arrived at the Neurology Department and spoke to the receptionist she was directed to the High Dependency ward where Ken lay connected up to monitors by an array of tubes and wires. She was shocked by how ill and diminished he looked. There was a dressing on his head and his blonde hair had been shaved to the scalp. His face had an unhealthy grey pallor with dark bruises beneath his closed eyes.

There were five other beds in the ward, two with privacy curtains pulled around them and the others had male patients who, like Ken, had similar tubes and wires connecting them to monitors. She stood by the side of the bed, looking down at Ken for several minutes. Her emotions in turmoil, her eyes filling with tears she tried to quell by bringing a handkerchief from her pocket and dabbing at her eyes. Her strength drained out of her and she quickly sat down on a high-back chair placed by the bed. She leaned across to him and involuntarily reached out to touch him as a wave of sympathy engulfed her. After a few minutes she leaned back, rested her head against the back of the chair and closed her eyes. Her thoughts hovered over last Friday events when she and Ken had rowed so bitterly.

It had started after they'd had breakfast and she was washing up. Ken had gone up to his bedroom to get ready for his trip to Manchester; he had moved out of their bedroom a fortnight back, accusing her of keeping him awake.

When he came back to the kitchen he had said without preamble, "There's a change of plan, I won't be back 'till Monday. Maybe even Tuesday."

She had turned from the sink. "What change of plan? You said the meeting would be today and you would be back tonight?"

"Like I said, change of plan. The Investors want more time to go over the project. Richard's just rung me." He held up his mobile with an irritable gesture.

Stung by his attitude and urged by her growing suspicions, she had blurted out, "Who is she?"

"What are you talking about, Clair?"

"This woman you are having an affair with?"

"Who the hell told you that? Your shitty sister, I suppose!"

"Don't you dare call Iris shitty!"

"Tart then. No, a shitty tart."

"Don't you dare use that language in this

house!"

"I'll use any bloody language I like!"

"You are disgusting. And you haven't answered my question. Are you having an affair?"

"If it wasn't your high and mighty sister, who then?"

"I worked it our for myself. Your attitude towards me has changed for a start. You've moved out of our bedroom. And...," she could feel a hot blush on her cheeks, "we don't have sex any more."

"Whose fault is that? You don't know the first thing about satisfying a man. You're a bloody prude."

"I told you not use that language. And don't you dare..." She never had chance to finish.

He had stepped forward and thrust his face an inch from hers, his hand caught hold of her blouse, twisting until it hurt her breast and his blue eyes had darkened with rage. "Dare! Don't you dare tell me what I can and can't do!"

The look on his face, the intensity of his eyes staring into hers had frightened her. She was struck dumb by this unsuspected side of her husband. She put her hand on his chest to push him away, but he had abruptly released her blouse and stepped back from her.

"Ah, to hell with you," he had said, swinging

away and storming out of the kitchen, and a few minutes later she heard him leaving the house.

She had been shocked to the core. She had never seen him in such a rage, and certainly never had an inkling he thought of her that way. From the moment they had met in late summer last year until six weeks ago, they seemed to have the perfect marriage. And when they had occasionally crossed words he would quickly make up. The gradual change in his character over last six weeks had worried her, making her wonder what she was doing wrong; but that terrible rage, so unexpected, like a volcano exploding, had frightened and horrified her and she had thought he'd do her physical harm. When he had stormed out, she had flopped down onto a kitchen chair. put her face in her hands and sobbed uncontrollably. Up until that moment she had loved him so deeply and truly that suddenly she had the frightening experience of looking into a psychological abyss where madness lurked.

She dragged her thoughts back to the present and opened her eyes, looked at Ken and she wondered if, like her, he'd stared into an abyss and driven his car deliberately off the road. No, she couldn't believe he had it in him to commit suicide, he was a fighter and too full of life and living it to the full. Maybe she had been wrong about the affair? Maybe listening to her sister telling her Ken was deceitful and a womaniser had made her jump to conclusions he was having an affair when his attitude had changed towards her? Was it business worries plaguing him? He had not admitted he was playing away. Maybe her accusation being false had sparked his uncontrollable temper against her and Iris. All she knew, seeing him so vulnerable, was that she still loved him. Iris was probably right in calling her a fool where Ken was concerned. But if it was business worries causing the change in his character then she was prepared to forgive those cruel words and make peace with him.

Her troubling thoughts were interrupted by a staff nurse pulling the privacy curtain around them. Her name tag read: "GILL". She gave Clair a quick smile. "I have to check Ken over, I'm afraid."

Clair stood up and made to leave.

"You can stay if you like, Mrs Birkenshaw. I'll not be long." She started checking the tubes and wires attached to Ken.

"Is he going to be all right? "He looks so ill."

Staff Nurse Gill stopped her checking to give Clair a reassuring smile. "He's improving every day, love. And he's in capable hands. Dr Miller is a very experienced Neurologist and he's pleased with your husband's progress."

"Thank you. You don't know how much those words mean to me. I only wish I could be of help in some way."

"Well, you can by talking to him or reading to him when you visit."

"What? Even when he can't hear me?"

"Oh, it's surprising how much unconscious patients can hear, Mrs Birkenshaw. And it's a well known that talking to them is helpful in their recovery."

Clair looked down at Ken. "Then that's what I'll do. Thank you again, Gill."

They smiled at each other and she waited until Gill had finished before sitting again. She placed her hand over Ken's and in a low voice began speaking. At first she felt uncomfortable she was talking to an unresponsive person, but by telling him how devastated she had been when hearing of his accident, her words had a calming affect on her, and she went on to tell him of her day and what she planned. When she looked at her watch a bit later she was surprised an hour had slipped away.

CHAPTER 3

In the dream he was eleven years old and filled with an overwhelming grief that tore at his heart. He couldn't stop the sobs, or the tears streaming down his face. They were in his aunt Alice's dining room and she had just told him his mum and dad had been killed in a plane crash on their way home from America. The grief turned to anger. He kicked at the oak table leg, shouting, "Not true! Not true!" He could feel his despair growing and engulfing him. He closed his eyes to stop the tears. He had no one. Nobody to tell him what a good lad he was. Nobody to shout from the sidelines when he scored a goal. Nobody to comfort him when he fell off his bike. Nobody to wipe away his tears when he couldn't stop them.

His aunt Alice told him he'd have to be brave and act like a man.

The dream skipped on, he had been staying with his aunt Alice while the authorities tried to place him with close relations. His maternal grandparents had refused point blank to have anything to do with him. His paternal grandfather, a widower and suffering from ill health was not suitable. Aunt Alice made it plain to the authorities her job as a school teacher left no time to look after an eleven old, especially one grieving so badly for his parents. Now he had been placed temporary in a Social Care Home. The place made him think of suicide...how to do it..?

He heard a voice breaking into his dream, pulling him away from the grief and the anger. He struggled to understand the words and half opened his eyes. Staff nurse Carole was looking down at him with the same sympathetic smile she had given him earlier this morning when she was assisting Dr Miller.

She touched his shoulder. "You were dreaming, Ken," she said. "Couldn't have been good, you were thrashing about and are those tears I see?"

He lifted a hand and wiped away the tears on his cheek. "No, it wasn't good."

"Hey, don't be embarrassed. love. It's probably all part of the recovery process. Come on, now. Time for your medication and blood pressure check." She pushed the hospital trolley closer to the bed. "Can't lie around doing nothing. Especially when your wife is visiting this afternoon."

There it was again, "Wife?" First he'd heard he had a wife was this morning when Dr Miller tried to kickstart his memory.

"Lovely lady." Nurse Carole continued. "She's been visiting every day. Talking to you even though you were so ignorant you pretended to be asleep." She laughed. He did not smile in return.

When she left he let random thoughts play around. Try as he might he couldn't remember a wife. He was just as confused as yesterday when he resurfaced from a four day coma and slipped into a half conscious state where shadowy figures leaned over him, asking unintelligible questions. He vaguely remembered someone sitting by the bed, holding his hand and talking to him in a quiet voice and he had drifted off to sleep wishing he could understand what she was saying.

Yesterday evening he had become fully conscious of his surroundings; found he had tubes inserted into his limbs and body to feed him fluids and drain fluids and wires attached to monitor his vital organs. When a nurse took his blood pressure and temperature he had asked where he was.

"HDU, Western General." she had said, before moving off to attend to the patient in the next bed. He hadn't a clue what HDU meant but he knew the Western General was in Sheffield.

A lady doctor had turned up to carry out an examination and ask if he was in any pain. He had mentioned the constant headache and general aches and pains, especially his ribs. After she had checked him over, she prescribed painkillers.

"What happened, Doctor?"

You had a car accident, Ken. Last Friday, and you've been in a coma for four days."

And here he was a day later still unable to remember anything before that damn car accident. And was his name Ken? It didn't feel right. God, he wished he could remember at least something. He touched the dressing on his head, wondering if his brain was seriously damaged. He found he was fighting off a panic attack. It was a living nightmare. He turned on his back, gazed up at the ceiling, looking for answers to his plight. The codeine started working, easing the pain in his head and he drifted into a half doze going over the morning events.

At 7am he suffered the embarrassment of having the catheter removed from his penis by a middle aged nurse. When she saw his anxious face, she said, "Don't worry, love. I've done more of these than you've had hot dinners."

8.30am, Two orderlies had turned up to wheel his bed out of the High Dependency Unit and into a private room. He had assumed it was normal hospital practice for recovering patients. The room was furnished with a single hospital bed, a bedside cabinet with a large jug of water and a plastic tumbler and a small digital clock standing on top. Two upright chairs were placed against one wall, and another chair which had a soft seat and wooden arms had been placed next to the bed.. There was a window next to the entrance door that had a roller blind which was closed. A large window on the opposite wall looked out onto a carpark surrounded by newly planted trees. Another door, in line with the end of his bed had been opened by one of the orderlies to show him the bathroom. There was a mobile emergency bell he could use if necessary.

At 9am he was brought out of a dreamless sleep by a voice saying, "Hi, Ken, I'm Barry and it's time for your bath, and we need to get you in that chair to change the bedlinen. Are you ok with that?" Barry was joined by Tina, who looked more like a sixth former than a trainee nurse.

What followed was an experience of painful movement as Barry helped him into the chair and Tina brought a bowl of warm water, a towel and a toilet bag. He felt the stubble on his chin and asked if he could have a razor. While he carried out his ablutions, Barry and Tina had given an exhibition on how to make a hospital bed.

Hardly had they gone when Dr Miller, his bald head shining, and his gold rimmed specs twinkling, turned up to prod and probe at his body and ask endless questions regarding Ken's life before the accident, which despite his best efforts, he had no recall. Nurse Carole had stood by, taking notes and looking sympathetic. Dr Miller had seemed pleased with the physical results and decided his medication and food could be taken orally instead of by drip. Finally he had contemplated Ken for a few seconds. "You seem to have regressive amnesia, Ken, which I don't think was caused by the head injury. The scans & EEG show no serious trauma to the brain and what little swelling occurred has gone down, leaving no discernible pressure. There could be other reasons for your memory loss.

"What other reasons?" he had asked.

"Stress is a common cause. And then there is the Ketamine and alcohol you had in your system, taken together they could cause a psychogenic disorder. If it persists I will arrange for you to see a specialist in amnesia." Dr Miller had changed the subject. "I understand your wife will be visiting you this afternoon..."

"Did you say, wife?" Ken interrupted.

Yes, that's right." He had consulted his notes. "Clair Birkenshaw. And when she visits I'll have a word with her to explain your condition. She could be a great help in recovering your memory."

The thought of a wife he couldn't remember caused Ken to have a sinking feeling in his stomach.

After the doctor, a physiotherapist, a small middle aged man with a grey beard trying to hide a large nose, came visiting and explained it was necessary to get patients walking again as soon as possible. He had brought a crutch with him. Those first tottering steps brought alive the aches and pains from the accident. But after ten minutes he felt confident to walk just using the crutch and without the assistance of the physiotherapist.

12pm. Lunch arrived by an orderly pushing a trolley and wearing a creased green overall and flip-flops saying, "No solids, love. Just soup, I'm afraid. Choice of drinks, coffee, tea, or orange juice."

And finally at one o'clock, it was Nurse Carole with the trolly and the medication and the sympathetic smile.

The medication she had given him was taking effect and he drifted off to sleep.

In the dream he was in the rest room of a Social Care Hostel. The room was large, and occupied with other boys, some of whom sat in various armchairs or at the three tables. Two boys were playing table tennis down the far end of the room, the click of the plastic ball being struck and the shouts of glee from the boys echoed off the cream walls. Three tall sash windows along one wall let in the evening light. He held a book in his left hand while staring out of a window at the drizzling rain. His second day as new boy and feeling as miserable as the weather outside. He had been nicknamed "Blondie" by the other boys because of his mop of blond hair, a name he hated because it sounded girlie, but life in the other care homes had taught him not to show his feelings.

He was startled out of his reverie by a push to his back. "Hey, Blondie, whatcha reading?"

He turned quickly to confront Garry Willman. His two mates stood just behind, grinning as Garry reached for the book: "Give us a look."

This was the third time Gary had tried baiting him to see how he would react. The first was at breakfast:

"Hey, Blondie," he had said taking a seat opposite at the table, while Kev and Rob, his two mates, had slipped into the remaining chairs.

He had carried on, buttering his toast, not afraid, and thought he could take them on one at a time or even two if necessary. He was big for his age and his father, who had been an amateur boxer up to his university days, had passed on his boxing skills. He pretended to ignored them, but Garry had been determined to get his attention.

"I think I need that more than you," he said, poking at the bowl of cornflakes on the table in front of them. Kev and Rob had nodded vigorously.

He had pushed the bowl towards Garry. "Have it, I'm not hungry."

They had stared at each other. Although Garry had a smile on his face, his grey eyes were hard and emotionless. Garry, was a good year older, but a fraction shorter. He had the brash confidence to take on any of the other boys in the hostel and he was now preparing to take on the newcomer.

One of his mates had reached for the bowl. "If you two don't want it, I'll have it."

Garry's hand had flashed, slapping Rob's wrist away from the bowl. He had not said a word, but continued to stare across the table for another few seconds before standing abruptly. "Nah, I'm not hungry either. Then he leaned down to whisper, "I'll see you later, Blondie. He had touched the blonde curls. "We'll give these a good cut, eh, then we can call you Baldie."

The three of them had walked off, laughing.

Another baiting had occurred at lunchtime. He had been passing Garry's table, carrying food back to his seat, when Garry's foot had shot out trying to trip him up. He had used his boxing skill and skipped aside to avoid the foot and carried on his way.

Now this, and the overwhelming anger and grief that had simmered over the past weeks and months, exploded out of control. He threw a vicious right hook hitting Gary in the chest just under the heart, causing his breath to whoosh out as he collapsed to the floor. Kev and Rob immediately laced in with fists flying. He dropped the book he'd been holding to defend himself and then attacked with such a ferocious flurry of blows causing Kev to to fall with blood streaming from his nose and Rob to turn his back and lean over, holding his stomach and moaning. Garry got his breath back, jumped to his feet and caught him in a choke hold, pulling him to the floor where they rolled about, each trying to get the upper hand. There was a shout and two strong arms pulled them apart. They struggled for a moment before realising it was the Superintendent holding them. They were marched to his office where they stood silent before him while he lectured on the hostel rules. Finally, he barked, "So, which of you started it?" And when they didn't speak. "If neither of you own up, you'll both receive punishment."

They looked at each other. Garry, a ghost of a smile around his lips and a hooded look to his eyes sent an unmistakable message. They looked up at the Superintendent and in unison said "It was me, Sir."

The dream began to fade, leaving him with the thought: It was at that precise moment he took the giant step from little boy to little man.

CHAPTER 4

Clair rang her sister to update Iris on Ken's condition. She knew Iris wasn't much interested in how Ken was progressing but she had to talk to her about the good news. "Ken has started to come out of the coma, sis. He opened his eyes yesterday and seemed to recognise me, and he gave my hand a squeeze when he saw me. And the tests are showing he's making good progress. Isn't that marvellous?"

"For your sake I suppose it is."

"Oh, come on. He's lucky to be alive. Why are you being so mean?"

"You know why, Clair. Ken Birkenshaw don't deserve you. He's a womaniser and probably cheating on you."

"Stop it, Iris. What happened between you and him was nearly eight months ago. He'd had too much to drink at the reception and so had you. And he did apologise.'

'You are so damned naive, Clair. It was your wedding day, remember. Talk about rose coloured glasses. You either won't or can't see him for what he is!'

"I'm not stupid, Iris. I know he has faults and

he can be rotten to me when he's in a temper." she said, recalling last Friday before Ken stormed out of the house.

"There you are, then. Why don't you divorce him. I know you'll be happier. You were before you married him."

"I'm not like you, Iris. You treat divorce as an easy come easy go option. Two in eight years speaks for itself. And another thing; we have only been married for eight months, it's too short a time to start thinking of divorce."

Iris, stung by Clair's mention of her failed marriages, said, 'Oh, have it your way. Just remember I warned you.'

Clair, wished she hadn't got into this pointless argument with her sister, she couldn't remember how many times Iris and she had argued over Ken. In an effort to lighten the mood she said, "Would like me to give him your regards?"

"Damn the regards, it's a kick up the backside I'd want to give him."

"It was a joke, Iris."

"I know, but I'm serious. He's a devious devil and there's something not right with that car accident."

"What do you mean. He was almost killed, Iris. You're becoming obsessed that he planned it.

Please, stop it. It's unhealthy, love."

"Have it your way, Clair. But I do wish you'd stop fooling yourself over that man."

Clair came off the phone wishing she'd not rung her sister.

Clair arrived at the hospital at 2pm and walked into the reception area of the Neurology Department and smiled at the receptionist, intending to walk on by as she had been doing since she first visited Ken, but she was stopped when the receptionist said, "Excuse me Mrs Birkenshaw but Dr Miller has left a note to say he'd like to see you before you visit your husband.

"Has something happed to Ken...my husband?"

"I shouldn't think so, Mrs Birkenshaw. Dr Miller would have let you know personally if there had been a dramatic change. Shall I let him know you are here."

"Yes, please."

The receptionist used the telephone and after a brief conversation, she said to Clair, "He'll see you now." She pointed to a corridor off the right. "At the end of that corridor, Mrs Birkenshaw. Name's on the door."

"Thank you."

Dr Miller greeted her by coming around his desk and shaking her hand. He was going bald, wore gold-rim spectacles and she noticed his middle age spread pushing hard against the buttons on his white coat.

"Take a seat , Mrs Birkenshaw," he said, motioning to the upright chair in front of his desk. She sat and he moved back behind his desk to sit in his swivel chair and direct his attention to her.

"I understand you were with your husband when he first regained consciousness yesterday," he said.

"That's right," Clair said, smiling. "I think he recognised me and he definitely squeezed my hand." She noticed the frown and he was not endorsing her good news. "He's not worse, is he?"

"Oh, no, Mrs Birkenshaw, the opposite in fact. The good news is your husband has fully regained consciousness since yesterday and we are pleased with his physical progress. The scans and the EEG show his brain has not suffered long term trauma and the swelling has now gone down."

"What then?"

Dr Miller didn't answer straight away, but glanced down at an open folder on his desk. He looked up and said, "The examinations and tests carried out on your husband are showing he has psychogenic amnesia. In other words he is having trouble remembering past events and even personal details such as his name or where he lives."

"That's terrible! So what's causing this psycho..."

"Psychogenic amnesia. It is generally the result of an emotional shock which causes the brain to block out certain information. It can also be caused by drugs, traces of which were found when he was admitted to A&E.

"The police also said that. But Ken never took drugs, and I told the police the same. What sort of drugs?"

"I'm sorry, Mrs Birkenshaw. We did find Ketamine as well as alcohol in his blood. And Ketamine can cause memory loss as well as confusion and several other unhealthy side effects."

"Ketamine? isn't that a date drug?"

"It can be used for that, yes." Doctor Miller showed his irritation at her questions by saying abruptly, "But the point I want to make is your husband may not recognise you when you visit and you will need patience for his memory to return."

"That can't be right! It's like I said, I'm sure he recognised me yesterday."

Dr Miller pursed his lips. "You could have

been mistaken, Mrs Birkenshaw."

Clair started to shake her head but suddenly remembered hearing of cases where people with memory loss had to be reminded of past events every day.. She felt queazy. "Does it mean he'll not remember me again today or tomorrow, or the day after?"

"No, no." Doctor Miller hastened to assure her. "That's anterograde amnesia. And he's not showing any signs of that since he regained consciousness. No, your husband has the symptoms of retrograde amnesia. Meaning he can't recall past events. And it is still early days." Dr Miller continued. "And he may recognise you when you see him, but don't be disappointed if his memory fails him. You may also notice a profound change in him. All I can say is familiar faces, surroundings or familiar objects all have the potential of triggering memory recall."

"What about photographs? Will they help? I have some wedding photos with me and also a few we took of our garden."

"Splendid. They could be of help, certainly."

Clair stood, she had the sudden urge to see Ken for herself. "Thank you for putting me in the picture, Doctor. But I think I'd like to see Ken now, please."

"Yes, of course, Mrs Birkenshaw," he said, rising from his chair, "Oh, and he's been moved to a private room as you requested. Same area as the HDU but down the corridor opposite."

"Thank you Doctor."

Then as Clair headed for the door, he said, "Try not to tire him too much. The more rest he has the quicker his recovery."

"I'll bear it mind, and thank you again."

CHAPTER 5

When he opened his eyes the digital clock read 14.50. While he slept someone had raised the blind on the observation window. A female face looked in at him. The door opened and a tall young woman with dark wavy hair down to her shoulders, smiled hesitantly, then walked over to give him a kiss on the cheek, and in a rush of breathy words said, "Hello, Ken. You've been giving us a hard time, you know. How are you? Are they looking after you?"

Ken assumed this was his wife and couldn't help studying her, noting her expressive brown eyes, her high cheekbones and the way her dark hair fell about her face when she leaned forward. She was a classic beauty. She wore a flowery, knee length dress that outlined her slim build. Her perfume was familiar. And he suddenly remembered her. "I know you," he blurted. "You were here yesterday, talking to me and holding my hand. "Her eyes lit up and her lips parted in a generous smile. But before she could say anything, he said, "But I can't remember you as my wife!"

Her eyes dimmed, the smile faded. She looked completely crushed and he wished he'd kept his mouth shut. In an effort to placate her, he said, "I'm sorry, but I really don't remember you from before the accident. I wish I hadn't confused you by mentioning yesterday."

Clair looked at him with tears in her eyes. "Oh, Ken. I'm so sorry..." Her voice tailed off and she spent a moment staring at him with a puzzled look before straightening up as if pulling herself together.

She turned to one of the upright chairs and pulled it to the bedside. Looked at him for another moment and sighed as she sat down. "I was so sure you had recognised me yesterday, Ken. I even told Dr Miller."

"All I can say again, Clair. I can call you, Clair...?"

She laughed out loud at the absurdity of his question "Oh! Ken. Don't be so daft. I'm your wife."

"Well I'm truly sorry for upsetting you. It wasn't my intention."

"Pointless for us to worry over it, darling. Better we try to get your memory back, don't you think?" She brought her shoulder bag around to her lap, dug inside and pulled out a 5"x7" photograph folder and handed it across. "Have a look. There's some photos from our wedding and a few others. If they don't jog your memory I don't know what will."

The first photo he looked at showed him and Clair on their wedding day. They were standing on the steps of a church, looking into each others eyes and smiling broadly. Clair looked absolutely gorgeous in a long white wedding gown and he was in a traditional morning suit. At first he couldn't believe it. But his blonde hair and the other facial features were unmistakably his. He was surprised how tall and burly he looked. He must have lost a lot of weight through the accident. He studied the photo for nearly a minute, hoping some memory of the day would come to him. Not a glimmer. The second photo was of the wedding group. Clair rose off the chair to sit on the bed where she was able to point out and give names to the guests.

She pointed to the figure standing next to her, "Iris, my sister, she was my bridesmaid. And that's Mum, looking very pleased with herself." He could see where Clair got her looks from. "Dad, on the end, he's a peach. Paid for the lot without a grumble." He was about the same height as Clair and slim with only a few flecks of grey at his temples. She brought her finger back to their images in the centre, let it rest there a moment, before looking at him, "Anything?" He shook his head. Disappointment clouded her eyes and she stared back at the photo. Moved her finger to the man standing next to him. "Your best-man, Josh. You and he go back a long way - university. Surely you remember him?" He heard the undertone of frustration in her voice. He remained quiet watching her finger resting on his best man. "Anyway, he lives in London now with Tina," she moved her finger to a blonde with shoulder length hair and a barbie doll face. She was wearing a dress so short it could have been worn as a blouse. "Wouldn't think she has an I.Q. of one-five-five would you? Works at one of those posh international banks, same as Josh."

He indicated the man with flowing white hair and ruddy face and the only one with a serious expression. "And is that my father on the end?"

"Father? No, that's Rickard Cartwright. He's a long term investor in your firm. You and he have done a lot of business together." Clair stared at him with sympathy. "You are an orphan, darling."

The memory of his dreams made him look inwards and he took his eyes away from the photo to gaze out the window at the carpark. He was beginning to sense a panic attack coming on, similar to the one he had fought off earlier in the day. He took several deep breaths before returning his attention to the next photo. They were standing in front of an enormous wedding cake, in close up and looking directly into the camera lens. Clair's eyes sparkled out of her perfectly made up face. He had a sardonic grin on his. He closed his eyes as a bunch of images flitted through his mind. They were a series of transparent images of himself with shadowy figures shimmering behind him. He shuddered and quickly put the photo back with the others and shoved them back in the folder.

He sucked in a long breath. "At least they show I am who you say I am."

"Of course they do, What did you expect?"

"I don't know, I genuinely thought I was some-one else."

"Oh, you are definitely Ken, Ken." They both laughed spontaneously, and his threatening panic attack receded.

Clair became serious. "I think I understand, darling. It must be devastating not to remember anything at all. What about when you were younger? Nothing there?"

"No, not really." He hesitated, wondering if he should mention the two dreams. He had been sure they were real scenes from his childhood and with Clair saying he was an orphan, the dreams could be of real events. He decided it was too early to say anything.

Clair's brown eyes softened showing her dis-appointment but she put on a brave smile.

He changed the subject. "How did we meet?"

"At a charity do. Ten and a half months ago. She laughed softly. "Funny really, it was to raise funds for this hospital. You had been one of the developers to get the project off the ground a few years previously. They wanted some expensive equipment which was outside the NHS budget."

"So what happened?"

"Well, we danced and fell in love and married two months later. The romantic clique." Another laugh. but laced with embarrassment, followed by an almost silent whisper. "At least I did."

She stood up abruptly and he was surprised how disappointed he was. He had been in the act of putting his hand over hers because he had suddenly felt a rush of sympathy for her.

"Dr Miller told me not to tire you too much. And I can see you are as disappointed as me by not remembering our wedding."

"Will I see you tomorrow."

"Of course. I want to know if you remember any of the photos. She hesitated then bent down and gave him a peck on the cheek. "See you tomorrow, darling."

"Bye," he said, as she waved from the doorway. He was sorry to see her leave. He closed his eyes, he had a headache and his thoughts became confused as they wandered over the discussion with Clair about his past. He had niggling doubts, despite all the photographic evidence, that she was his wife. He would have remembered her, surely?

He opened his eyes and reached for the folder of photographs. He looked again at the wedding photos. His eyes lingered on the group photograph. As he studied it the image blurred and morphed into a scene of a restaurant. The scene solidified. He was sitting opposite a woman with blonde curly hair, soft red lips and wearing a low-cut dress showing a deep cleavage. She held a fluted wine glass up and smiled broadly, showing Hollywood white teeth. She leaned across the table and puffed out her lips as if to give him a kiss and then began to shimmer as the scene faded and he was looking at the wedding image once more. He was sweating. His mind on the edge of panic. His breath shallow and fast. He mentally fought to get control and eventually succeeded. But it left him drained and limp and slipping into an exhausted sleep.

When Clair left Ken's room her emotions were all over the place. Despite Dr Miller's warning that Ken's memory loss could have a profound effect on his character, she had not been prepared for the striking difference. He had been so vulnerable, so lost and with a reserve that made him almost untouchable. Several times she had wanted to comfort him and had almost reached out, especially when she saw panic in those extraordinary blue eyes when he couldn't remember their wedding. Even when they had laughed at themselves in a moment of togetherness she had stopped herself from touching him, waiting for him to make the first move. But he hadn't, and she realised as she walked along the corridor he was not the overconfident Ken he had been before the accident. And she couldn't make up her mind if that was a bad or a good thing.

She also noticed he had lost quite a lot of weight, well over a stone and she put it down to him receiving liquid nourishment instead of solid food. He was going to find his clothes hanging on him unless he put on some more weight.

When she arrived home and contacted Iris to tell her Ken's condition and behaviour, saying how much he had changed, Iris had actually snorted.

"Memory loss?" You sure he's not faking it, Clair?"

"Don't be so absurd, Iris! You should've seen him. He was panicked and in distress when I showed him our wedding photographs. And Dr Miller is convinced Ken has amnesia."

"Well, I would take it with pinch of salt, love. Your Ken could convince a bird it was a butterfly."

Clair was so upset with her sister, she put the phone down on her. Something she hadn't done since they were teenagers.

She rang her parents, who lived in Eastbourne. They had moved there when her dad had retired early from his solicitor business. She spoke to her father, her mother had gone to one of her craft clubs.

"Glad to hear he's making progress, sweetheart," he said, when she had finished updating him. "I have heard of Dr Miller, he is considered a top notch neurologist, I'm sure he'll do the very best for him. And don't listen to Iris. You know how she dislikes Ken. Would you like me to pop up?" He didn't sound enthusiastic.

Clair knew her father hated the journey. "No need, Dad. There's nothing you could do, anyway."

Iris sighed when Clair slammed the phone down on her. She shouldn't have snorted and ridiculing Birkenshaw had been a step too far, especially with Clair in a fragile emotional state after learning Birkenshaw had suffered a serious trauma during the car accident. It had been wrong of her and she should be thinking more of Clair's state of mind. Clair was right to say her hate had become an obsession against her husband. She had to admit when hearing Constable Turner's news that Birkenshaw was seriously injured in a car accident, her heart had leapt with joy and she had wished he would not recover. But now he was on the road to recovery. Yes, she thought, it was a great pity he hadn't died when the car exploded.

But by pushing so hard to convince her young sister to stop looking at Ken Birkenshaw with romantic eyes, and to end her relationship with the deceiving conniving bastard she was in fact causing a rift to open up between them. But how else to save her sister from a looming emotional disaster. Clair was a born romantic and Iris knew deep down her sister would go on loving the man to the bitter end. On the one hand she loved her sister for being the most loyal, trusting and affectionate person anyone could meet. On the other hand it was so frustrating when those traits had made it easy for a charmer like Birkenshaw to weasel his way into Clair's heart and blind her to his true deceitful character. Even when she told Clair of the uninvited kiss and his attempt to have sex with her, Clair had still refused to believe it was other than Birkenshaw reading the signals wrong and accusing her of being equally to blame. And Clair had insisted the apology from Birkenshaw should be the end of the matter. The galling outcome of that attempt to open Clair's eyes to the treacherous nature of her husband had resulted in Clair believing him and not her. God, fancy Clair trusting him instead of her. She had always looked out for her little sister, being there to support and comfort when Clair had suffered emotionally and physically from the wars of life's events. Yet, here was a rotten bastard able to walk into their lives and break their sisterly bond apart.

Thinking back she realised he had fooled even her when Clair had introduced him at the engagement party. He was handsome, with flowing blonde hair and magnetic blue eyes which made even her heart flutter. On top of the visual attributes he was witty, jovial and attentive. He certainly knew how to trap a woman with his charm and charisma. Yes, he had fooled her good and proper. But not for long. She was not the naive romantic, nor an innocent like her sister. She had been married twice, knew the sexual dating game backwards, and Birkenshaw, like all sexual predators, had to see how far he could advance into her personal space; the touch to the arm, the shoulder, the hair and the odd body to body brush, accidentally of course. The accompanying cheeky grin or the inquisitive gaze. And what she found infuriating he was quite blatant in making it obvious to her that he was available if she so wished. She had in those early days tried to convince Clair that Ken Birkenshaw was not to be trusted, he was a womaniser, she had said. He was the wrong man for her and he would break her heart. But her advice had failed to release Clair's captured heart and all Iris could do was curse the day her innocent sister had met and fallen under the bewitching spell cast by that devil incarnate Now all she could do was be available when Clair came to her senses and if any long-term emotional harm was inflicted by Birkenshaw, she would make certain he was brought to book, even if she had to kill him herself.

CHAPTER 6

For the next week Clair visited Ken every day, showing different photos or telling him about his life before the accident. He had fallen into the habit of studying each photograph in minute detail, hoping he might recognise a slither of something. He also listened attentively when she talked about events before his accident, only occasionally asking a question. His reserve faded and they conversed with growing ease. Clair secretly began to hope Ken wouldn't change back to his old self when he regained his memory. Before the accident, and despite how charming he could be, he had always been self-centred, self-opinionated and he was the boss. Now he seemed to be more interested in her than himself. Asking about her family. And when she told him her mum and dad had retired to Eastbourne and Iris was her only sibling and was five years older than her, Ken had listened by keeping eye contact which somehow made her feel important to him and encouraged her to open up as she never did before.

She told him they lived in a converted old farmhouse on the edge of the Peak District and it had belonged to her parents but her father had deeded it to her on her wedding day, provided she kept it in her name only because it was part of her inheritance. There was a marked difference in his reaction to this bit of news to when she explained it to him after they were married. Then he'd been cross, saying they should share everything because they were married. But now he said, "Good thinking." and smiled as if understanding her father's wishes.

As the week wore on his physical condition improved and using the metal crutch he walked the corridors, increasing the pace as the days went by. The sutures sealing the wound on his head were removed, and his blonde hair became a fuzz on his scalp. By the end of the week he had dispensed with the crutch, and his stature took on his broad shouldered stance she had so admired when she first met him.

The miserable weather of March was replaced by the budding Spring of April with the persistent grey skies opening into blue for the sun to shine down, and they were able to stroll in the hospital gardens. They were sitting on one of the garden benches when he finally told her of his dreams which were regular and seemingly more real than the reality of the hospital. His mention of his mother and father being killed in a plane, prompted her to say, "You've never really talked about your parents, Ken. Just said you were an orphan from an early age. And the only time you did mention them was when someone asked if you had ever taken drugs. And you said, never, because your mother and stepfather had taken them regularly. You actually used to get cross when I asked for more information about your early years. And in the end I just stopped asking."

Her description of his parents seemed to differ from the way his dream had portrayed them. He wondered if he really had an aunt Alice or if she was just a figment of his imagination. He could feel reality slipping away and he took several deep breaths to fight off a panic attack.

She saw the confusion and panic drift into his eyes, and she immediately reached out to grip his hand and suggest they waited to see what Dr Miller had to say.

When Ken described his dreams to Dr Miller and wondered if they could be versions of real events. Dr Miller, had frowned, saying they may be of real events from his childhood, but cautioned him again that one of the symptoms with psychogenic disorder was a tendency for patients to create false events and personal information. During the meeting he arranged an appointment for Ken to see a psychiatrist in a fortnight's time.

The following Monday, after his usual medical examination, Dr Miller told Ken he would be free to leave the hospital the following day. Adding, "Considering the physical trauma you've suffered, Ken, your recovery has been remarkable. I put it down to your excellent health before the car accident."

"I think I had a regular morning exercise regime before the accident, Doctor," Ken replied. He then related how each morning, before the breakfast trolley sounded in the corridor outside, he rose from the bed and went through a series of exercises; touching his toes, squats, stretches, and also floor routines; press-ups, and stomach exercises, etc. He carried out the routines by rote, as if it had been something he'd done before the accident, something remembered in his subconsciousness.

"You could be right," Doctor Miller said, "Whatever the reason, you've done well."

Ken told Clair the news when she visited that afternoon. The fact she was pleased gave a sparkle to her brown eyes and a smile to her lips that dimpled her cheeks, urging Ken to lean forward and kiss her lightly on her forehead. "There are times, young lady when you make me feel like a kid again."

"Give over, Ken Birkenshaw," Clair said, smiling and felt a rush of happiness she hadn't had for a long time.

CHAPTER 7

The next day Clair brought a case to the hospital filled with a selection of Ken's casual clothes. She watched for a minute as he picked through the case, lifting t-shirts, then putting them down, picking up a pair of trousers, frowning at it and putting it back in the case. She stepped forward and said, "Here, let me love," and chose the clothes for him.

She saw he was embarrassed to dress in front of her so she made an excuse to leave the room and returned ten minutes later.

The pale blue t-shirt and beige chinos suited his colouring and when he looked at her with a sardonic grin she felt the same flutter in her heart as when she first saw him across that dance floor. She was pleased to see the clothes fitted him reasonably despite his weight loss. He must be putting some back on she thought.

Clair repacked the case and made to carry it but he took it from her and they walked out to the car park side-by-side. Clair opened the boot of her Honda Civic and he put the case inside. As he walked to the passenger door he started to feel lightheaded and was glad to get in the car. Clair started the engine and he glanced across at her.

Suddenly her features started to blur and morph into the same blonde woman he'd seen when he had looked at the wedding photo. He felt the familiar panic attack quicken his heart. The blonde woman smiled with a hidden meaning. It was not a nice smile. The blood drained from his face. He had the horrible sensation of starting to fall into an abyss. Then a voice calling. Clair's voice...

"Ken? Ken! What's wrong!" He could feel the weight of her hand on his arm and his head began to clear, the image of the blonde woman faded and Clair was staring at him, her face etched with frightened concern.

His smile was feeble, the muscles on his face unfreezing from the grimace of horror that had overwhelmed him. He squeezed her hand. "I'm ok now. I just had one of those visions I told you about. This time her face was imposed over yours..."

"I think we should go back inside, love. Your face is white and you are shaking."

"No, I don't want to do that, sweetheart. I'm fine, honest."

Clair stared at him, shook her head in frustration and put the car into gear.

The old farmhouse was at the end of a short drive and Ken gazed at it as Clair pulled to a stop near the front door. When he stepped out of the car, he stretched and walked over to the low fence to admire the view of the wooded valley sloping down to the village of Millward a couple of miles distant. Clair walked over and stood beside him.

"Great view," he said, before turning to make eye contact with her. "Yes, I must admit, great views around this part of the world."

Clair give him a gentle dig in the ribs with her elbow, "Come on, I'll show you the house. Don't forget the case."

He collected the case from the car and as Clair dug around in her bag for the front door key, he admired the ornamental brass bell push.

Clair noticed out of the corner of her eye. "Remember it?"

"No, sorry."

"Don't apologise, Ken, I've more or less given up for now," she said, opening the door and leading the way inside. "It's like Dr Miller said, we just have to be patient. Leave the case while I show you around downstairs."

They did a quick tour of the ground floor: dining room, loo, garden room, "It's what we call it, but Mum refers to it as the sitting room when she visits." Clair said, and carried on to the kitchen, where, with an encompassing gesture said, "And this is my domain, most of the time. Come on I'll show you where your den is and the gym and my workshop."

She led him back down the inner hall to a fourteen foot square room furnished with a small oak desk, an executive leather swivel chair, a tall bookcase filled with books on a variety of subjects from business to golf to fishing and sporting guns. Against the left hand wall, a metal filing cabinet. A window behind the desk threw sunlight onto a silver coloured laptop sitting in the middle of the desk. There were no ornaments or flowers. Obviously a macho male domain. Ken wondered how many hours he'd sat at that desk, scheming on how to make his next million. He motioned to the desk. "Do you mind?"

"You don't have to ask. It's all yours, Ken."

He moved into the room and sat in the chair, swinging it slightly left to right, getting the feel of it. Clair came into the room and stood to one side of the desk. He pulled the laptop toward him, opened the lid and switched it on. For the first time since waking from the coma he felt at ease with what he was doing. His fingers raced over the keyboard without thought. It fired up and asked for a password. He pressed the return key on the off chance no password had been set. The screen changed and the desktop screen showed the dock along the bottom with various icons. Over the next few minutes he highlighted icons, brought up different screens he quickly examined, moved on until he finally shut down the computer and said, "It's only a month old, has no password, no sensitive information, just a few business letters and some contacts info. There must be another computer I used, or maybe a tablet."

Clair frowned. "I don't know, Ken. You never discussed your business dealings with me. And this is the first time I've entered this room with you. Normally it is only to clean it. That computer looks like the one you used regularly. Maybe it broke down and you had to replace it."

He wasn't convinced and started opening the desk drawers. Most were empty and only one contained some old folders with backdated correspondence. While he was searching the desk, Clair looked in the filing cabinet. Every drawer was empty.

"Strange," Clair commented. "Why would you want a filing cabinet if you don't use it."

"Do I have an office in town?"

"You did up to last month. Then you closed it down saying Richard had offered you office space in his building. Made sense if you were to save money on office rent. You could check with him."

"Well, it's not urgent at the moment."

Clair nodded agreement and kept quiet about

Richard Cartwright ringing several times to ask if Ken had recovered his memory. Her husband needed peace and quiet for now, she thought.

"Come on then," she said, "I'll show you the other two rooms on this floor."

He followed her through a door at the end of the hall and into a two room modern extension. Clair explained it had been added to the old farmhouse just before they were married. A gym had been set up in one room and kitted out with expensive exercise machines. "No wonder you looked so fit, Clair," Ken said, with a grin.

Clair rolled her eyes making Ken laugh. For a moment she looked like a teenager. "We used to work out together when we first got married. But it only lasted a couple of weeks. Then you said you didn't have the time and that running a business was all the workout you needed." There was an undertone of bitterness.

He almost mentioned his morning exercise routine but kept quiet about it. It was another of those differences between his lifestyle before the car accident as portrayed by Clair and his own subconscious reality. And until his memory returned and he could recall events for himself then he wouldn't know for certain what was real and what was false.

The other room was her workshop. A heavy

a duty work bench was placed under a large window and several pieces of jewellery, work in progress by the look of them, were scattered over the top, glittering in a shaft of sunlight. A miniature kiln sat next the bench. A smaller worktable was up against another wall with a swivel typist chair in front; and against the opposite wall, an old double kitchen unit with a large vase of garden flowers placed in the centre. Ken walked over to the bench and studied the jewellery without picking any up. He turned to look at her. "You really are a clever girl, young Clair."

Clair shrugged at the compliment, remembering the last time he came into the this room and said she was wasting her time. She led the way back to where they'd left the case. She picked it up. "There's the upstairs," she said.

He reached across and took the case from her. "Lead on, McDuff."

Clair opened the door to the first room at the top of the stairs, "Our main bedroom. And up until a few weeks before the accident we slept together," Her cheeks were turning pink.

"Had we fallen out?" he said, giving the room a quick once over. King-size bed, with a rather worn teddy bear on one of the silk pillows, glass topped bedside tables, a long wardrobe filling one wall, and a framed watercolour of a country village dominated by an old Norman church. Wooden floors with fluffy white throw rugs either side of the bed.

"You were falling out with me, Ken. And I might as well tell you now." He saw her take a deep breath. "I am not certain, but I think you were having an affair. You had changed over the last few months, short tempered and secretive. Now I don't know. It could have been work." She made eye contact and stared at him for several seconds, her brown eyes showing troubled thoughts.

She turned away and said, "Bring the case." She walked out of the bedroom.

Ken followed with the case, knowing he'd hurt her badly when he'd moved out and wishing he could remember why he'd made the decision.

"Bathroom." She indicated a door as they passed, but didn't stop until she reached the next door and opened it. "Your room, Ken Birkenshaw."

He put the case down and looked around the room: Double bed, neatly made with a bedside unit either side, double white wardrobe against one wall, mirrored dressing table also white, two unpainted basket chairs, and a bare wooden floor.

"I'll leave you to unpack and have a look around while I prepare our evening meal."

Clair walked downstairs, mentally kicking

herself for being short tempered with Ken. She had forgotten for the moment Dr Miller's words of caution and the advice to be patient. She had harked back to their relationship before the car accident. To when he was the old Ken, to a time he couldn't remember and it had been totally unfair of her to saddle him with her hurt and anger, even if he was the original cause of it. By the time she reached the kitchen she had decided their first full meal together since the accident would be something special.

Ken used the en suite to shower and shave. He studied his face in bathroom mirror for a few moments before getting dressed. The scar was healing nicely and the fuze covering his head had almost hidden it. The bruising under his eyes had disappeared and his fair skin had taken on a healthy tone. Pity his brain refused to release his past. He searched through the wardrobe and the chest of drawers, choosing what to wear. He dressed in another pair of chinos and a white t-shirt and a comfortable pair of slippers he found under the bed before heading downstairs.

The smell of food cooking drew him towards the kitchen and he paused in the doorway to admire Clair. She stood at the stove, using a large wooden spoon to taste whatever she was cooking. The material of her dress clung to her slim figure and showed off her subtle curves. She was wearing an apron, tied at the back to protect her dress and she had pulled the glossy black hair into a loose pony tail, showing off the delightful curve of her neck.

The smell of cooking meat from the stove made his stomach rumble. He hadn't realised just how hungry he was. He coughed gently to catch her attention. She turned, the wooden spoon held like a baton, her dark brown eyes sparkling, reflecting the light from the overhead electric lamps.

"You look smart, Ken," she said with a smile. And he knew they were friends again.

"Smells good. Can I help?"

"No, I have everything covered. There's a glass of wine over there," she said, pointing the spoon to the countertop in the far corner. "It's a red you like. Go and sit down, I'll call you when I'm ready."

He turned to leave and noticed the table top and the jewellery designs Clair had been looking at before she started cooking. He walked over and looked at the top sheets. "Are these the designs you told me about, Clair?"

She glanced across and saw what he was looking at. "Yes, those are my latest designs. Haven't had a chance to start making the jewellery yet."

"Well, I can see from these drawings you are a good artist. Do you paint?"

"Occasionally. Now off you go before something starts burning."

Later, when they were eating the meal in the dining room, with the candles giving a romantic glow, Ken complemented Clair on her cooking. "This steak is delicious. Probably the best I've ever had."

"How do you know, love? If you can't remember your past." Clair was smiling to take the edge off her words.

"I did say, probably. Anyway, I think you are a damn fine cook."

They finished the meal and Ken helped to load the server trolley Clair had used to cart the food from the kitchen. But she refused to let him take the trolley back, insisting he take his last glass of wine through to the garden room and she would bring the coffee through when she had finished tidying up.

She was stacking the dishes in the dishwasher when it suddenly dawned on her the meal had been a success. Ken had not only complimented her cooking but had listened intently when she explained her hopes on building up a successful online business, selling her costume jewellery. He had suddenly been encouraging about her using the internet, saying an enticing website could make a huge difference. His enthusiasm for her business had encouraged her to reveal her budding ambitions, something she had kept from the old Ken. And when this thought entered her head it triggered the maddening conundrum of how new Ken could be so different from the old Ken. Stop it, Clair! she muttered to herself. Just enjoy the new Ken for what he is now! And with that thought she made the coffee.

It was getting dark when Ken entered the garden room and he found the switch to turn on the defused wall lights, giving the room a pleasant glow. He sat on the settee and put his feet up on a pouffe. The meal had made him sleepy and he closed his eyes intending just to relax until Clair brought in the coffee.

In the dream he sat in front of a twenty-seven inch computer screen, his hands were resting on a keyboard. A video game had been set up. He hit a few keys and the screen flashed with a virtual figure of a man wearing metal body armour that rippled when he flexed his bulging muscles. He hit a few more keys and KINSMAN in gothic script started flashing red, amber and green across the now running figure. He stopped the video and then replayed it several times. The title and the run into the game played perfectly every time. He had a feeling of satisfaction, of finally achieving a goal he'd been aiming at for some time. He was about to close the computer down when there was the sound of a doorbell, and he hit a key to blank the screen before answering the door. When he opened the door there was no one there, just an empty hall, unaccountably dark, and he sensed an aura of menace lurking in the shadows. He tried to push the door shut but it wouldn't move and a feeling of dread slipped into his mind. The room started to darken and he sensed a presence behind him. So real he shivered.

A hand on this shoulder, a gentle shake, "Ken?" His eyes opened to see Clair leaning over him, concern etching her face. And for a moment he was confused between the dream and reality. Gasping for breath, his heart racing so hard he thought it was going to burst.

"You were dreaming again, love. More like a nightmare by the way you were twitching. Are you all right?"

Relief flooded through him. His heart rate slowed. He took a deep breath and finally, took his feet off the pouffe and sat up. "Yes, thanks for waking me. Is that coffee I smell?" Making light of how frightened and confused he'd been.

She organised coffee for them both before asking, "Care to tell me what it was about?"

He related the dream and then shrugged his shoulders. "First time I've had that dream and like the others it seemed so real. But unlike the others this one was a nightmare and frightening."

"I wonder if it could be the drugs you had before the accident, Ken. Dr Miller said Ketamine had some nasty side effects, hallucinations and confusion as well as memory loss being some of them."

"Maybe, Anyway I'd like to forget it for now."

"What about TV? We have several box sets as well as films. And I always find a film with a good ending is just the antidote for depression."

"I'll take your word for it," he said with a grin. What do you suggest?"

Clair walked over to the TV unit and rummaged around in the unit drawer until she found the DVD she wanted. She inserted it in the recorder and came back with a remote control in her hand, plumped herself on the settee next to him and used the remote to set up the DVD, "One of my favourites, stupid, I know, but 'Love Actually' has so many little love stories and they all have a happy ending, it just makes me feel good inside." She decided not to say he used to tell her to stop being such a romantic and start living in the real world . Best he didn't know she only watched this film when he wasn't around.

"Can't remember it," he said with a smile, and settled back to be entertained.

About halfway through the film they found

themselves sitting close to each other. Ken's arm was around her shoulders and she had her head resting on his chest. The film had created an aura of romance they shared in silence. The film ended and Clair lifted her head to ask if he'd enjoyed it, but his lips on hers changed her mind. The kiss blossomed into fiery passion and then to clothes shed with miraculous ease, and the settee became a bed of breathless and exhausted consummation. When passion was spent, Ken held Clair in a gentle embrace, his face buried in the perfume of her hair.

Clair, lay in his arms, a warm, contented sensation holding her in awe. Old Ken had never ever made her feel this way. The indescribable emotion flowed through her body and consciousness made her love for new Ken fresh and unbelievably strong.

Later, when they went upstairs, they used the king-size bed to renew their lovemaking.

CHAPTER 8

The following morning sunbeams streamed through the kitchen window, splashed around the room and seemed to be a reflection of the happiness shimmering in Clair's heart. She hummed to herself as she prepared scramble eggs on toast and was about to call Ken when he appeared at the door, dressed in beige chinos and a sky blue shirt matching his eyes.

He came over and kissed her lightly on the lips. "Thanks for last night sweetheart," he said smiling broadly.

She had the hot saucepan in her hand, so she bumped him with her hip, her emotions making her eyes twinkle. "Think nothing of it, big boy. Now sit down and behave yourself." She turned away to put the scrambled eggs on the toast. She put the plates on the table and sat opposite him. They grinned at each other, unable to contain their emotions.

After breakfast Clair shooed Ken out of the kitchen, put the dishes in the dishwasher, poured coffee from the machine into large cups and took them through to the garden room. Ken had plonked himself in one of the armchairs but rose quickly to take the cups from her and place them on the low table between the two armchairs. Clair stared at him intently, the way he had unconsciously helped her with the coffee caused her to remember how often in the past he had let her wait on him without offering to help. She frowned, her doubts resurfaced making her wonder again at the dramatic change in his character. And then she remembered Dr Miller's caution that patients suffering with a psychogenic disorder could create another persona for themselves.

The ring of the telephone thankfully interrupted her thoughts and she stood up quickly to answer it,

"Hello, Richard. Well, yes., he is home. The hospital released him yesterday but he's not fully recovered." She looked across at Ken. He raised an eyebrow. She grimaced at him, then continued speaking into the phone. "Well, if you insist Richard, but I don't know what good it will do. Ken still hasn't recovered his memory."

"Alright, two o'clock will be fine."

She put phone the back in the cradle, shrugged at Ken and sat down again. "That was Richard Cartwright, He's rung several times since your accident and each time he has been more concerned over the loss of your memory. I've agreed he can see you this afternoon."

"I could have spoken to him myself. No need

to be so protective, Clair."

"I only tried to put him off because I can't see the point of him asking you a lot of questions if you can't remember anything. Anyway, he wants to speak to you face to face." She plonked herself down in the armchair, annoyance fading when he smiled at her.

"I'm sorry to be critical, sweetheart. I know you are only trying to do the best for me," he said.

She accepted his apology, picked up her cup of coffee and took a sip. "Thank you," she said.

Ken gazed at the outside world, where a few white clouds sailed across the blue sky. He wondered where they were off to and wished his life was as simple.

Richard Cartwright arrived on the dot, his silver grey hair had been barbered with expensive scissors. He wore a grey pinstripe suit, an unsmiling face and carried a leather briefcase. He accepted the peck on the cheek from Clair when she greeted him, but hesitated before accepting the offered handshake from Ken. Clair took them through to the dining room where she offered Richard something to drink. He shook his head, his grey eyes cold and unfriendly.

The room contained a dining table long enough to accommodate three chairs either side and one on each end. A long sideboard was graced with a large green vase on top. Against the opposite wall a squat drinks cabinet and, on the wall over it, a water colour painting, depicting a number of racing yachts. The furniture was matching pale beech-wood and caught the afternoon sunshine allowed in through single tall window.

"Do you mind if I speak to Ken alone, Clair."

Clair had already decided she would stay to make sure Richard would not bombard Ken with questions he could not answer. "That's not going to happen, I'm afraid. I told you on the phone, Ken is still recovering mentally from the trauma of the accident. If I see you are upsetting him then you will have to leave."

Cartwright tightened his lips into a thin line, while he stared at Clair, debating whether to accept her conditions. Finally, "As you wish. But I want your assurance what is said in this room, remains in this room."

Clair nodded, looked at Ken, who said, with a straight face, "As you wish."

Despite the tense atmosphere, Clair almost smiled as she motioned Cartwright to sit. She and Ken sat together opposite.

Cartwright put his briefcase on the table as he sat down and stared intently at Ken for almost a minute, assessing every inch of his face. "It's fair to tell you, Ken, I've made inquiries at the hospital as to your condition. But Doctor Miller was not forthcoming. He would not even confirm you had amnesia on the grounds a patient's medical records are private. I have ..."

"That"s a blinking cheek, Richard!" Clair interrupted. "I told you how serious Ken's trauma was. Why don't you believe me?"

Cartwright gave Clair a hard stare. "I have a damn good reason." He looked at Ken, "I have also spoken to the police about your accident. They were a bit more helpful, but not much. They told me it is still being investigated and any information I could supply regarding your mental state before the accident would be welcome. I've promised to get back to them."

"And what can you tell them that I can't!" Clair said.

"Oh for goodness sake, Clair! Just listen, will you!" He opened his briefcase and took out a sheaf of papers, glanced through the top three and pushed them across the table to where Ken was sitting. "Do you remember putting your signature to that contract, Ken?"

Ken looked at the papers, shuffling them twice over. The papers were photocopies of a contract for a development project on the outskirts of Manchester and ran into millions of pounds. Against his name the sum of five million had been inked in, and against Richard's, seven million. There were ten other names on the contract, with various sterling figures against each one. The total was fifty-three million.

Cartwright, his posture stiff and unyielding, never took his eyes off Ken while he was studying the papers.

Finally, Ken pushed the papers over to Clair, said "No, I don't remember seeing them, Richard."

Cartwright's stiff posture seemed to collapse like sailcloth shedding wind. His face turned white. Clair and Ken hardly heard the whispered, "Where's the bloody money, Ken?"

Ken shrugged his shoulders, "Sorry, I can't help you."

"Stop being so fu... For christ sake, man. Don't you realise you could be convicted of fraud! Spend years in prison."

Clair looked up from the papers she had been reading and glared at Richard. "Fraud? Don't you dare threaten us with fraud. The money will still be in the development account. And if you need Ken to access it you will have to be patient and wait for his memory to return."

Cartwright's lip curled, his eyes aflame with anger. "It's not there. It's an online account and he," stabbing his forefinger at Ken," has moved it to another account A bloody offshore account in his name."

"Oh, god!" Clair looked at Ken.

"Wouldn't the bank have queried it? That amount of money going abroad?" Ken said.

Cartwright didn't answer straight away, guilt flitted across his face before he hid it with a grunt. "We have a long standing arrangement with the bank."

"You've done it before!" Clair said, leaning across the table, her anger equal to his.

"That's not the point, and we have always used a business account with individual passwords from each of us before any large transactions took place. He must have used mine as well as his own."

Ken glanced at Clair, but she had gone quiet with a far away look in her eyes.

Ken frowned at Cartwright. "Are you saying you were careless with your security arrangements and I was able to access your passwords?"

"My security arrangements are fine. You're a slippery bastard, Birkenshaw, and you must have remembered my passwords when we worked together on the project."

Ken sighed. "Well, I'm really sorry I can't remember anything from before the accident. So what do you intend to do?"

"I will give you the next two days to get the money back where it belongs. If you refuse, I will inform the police." He saw concern on Ken's face. "I'm sorry, Ken. We have worked a good many years together, and I can't afford to let you get away with this if you are not going to come clean." He leaned across the table and pulled the copy contract from under Clair's hands and put it in his briefcase.

"You really don't believe I have amnesia, do you." Ken's voice showed his growing concern.

Cartwright stood up, pulled at his jacket to straighten it, before giving Ken his answer. "I've known you a good many years, Ken, as a friend and business partner and I know you better than anyone. And to be honest you can be a devious bastard when there's an extra mil. to be made."

He nodded to Clair, who had remained seated, tears making her brown eyes glisten, her hands, resting on the table showed her fingers weaved together so tight the knuckles glowed white.

When Cartwright left the room Ken turned to Clair. "Is he right, sweetheart? Am I such a villain. Could I do what he's accused me of?"

Clair turned her tearstained face towards him. "Oh! Ken. I wish I knew. First, Iris thinks you are the most deceitful man she's ever met, and now

Richard is saying the same. But unlike them I know for certain you do have a memory disorder. And Dr Miller is convinced too. And I don't think he's easily fooled."

"Thank's for that."

"I'm not finished yet," Clair snapped. "But taking all those millions from your business partners, I now think you are capable of that." She rose from her chair and almost ran from the room.

Ken remained seated, his gaze unfocused as his thoughts turned inward, trying to find answers to his growing confusion, and the frustration of relying on other people for a character assessment. Gradually, as he replayed all the events since he regained consciousness, there bubbled up from his core being, his mortal soul, that he could not be such a villain. He was convinced he could not steal from other people, whether they be friends, colleagues or even someone he despised, and he suddenly realised he actually despised Richard Cartwright, and even more bizarre he despised himself, Ken Birkenshaw.

His only hope would be the return of his memory so he could put things right.

CHAPTER 9

When Clair left the room she went to the bathroom to wash her face and put fresh makeup on. She couldn't tidy up her thoughts though. They were in turmoil and she fought an inward battle to make sense of it all. Was Ken guilty of stealing that money? Based on the evidence presented by Richard Cartwright the answer had to be 'Yes'. Was he pretending to have lost his memory? A definite 'No'. And the real crunch question, was the new Ken going to return to the old Ken when his memory returned? A question she really couldn't answer. A question that was doing her head in. But the thought of him going to prison, old Ken or new Ken almost brought on a flood of tears again. She took several deep breaths, glared at herself in the bathroom mirror, gritted her teeth and steeled herself to be strong willed. She left the bathroom with dry eyes, but a lump in her throat. She changed out of the blouse she'd been wearing and put on a cashmere cardigan over the clean pink blouse. She left her black slimline slacks on and dug out a pair of thick walking socks from the bottom drawer of her dresser.

Ken met her in the kitchen. They made eye contact but the atmosphere between them mirrored their troubled thoughts.

"I need some fresh air," Clair announced abruptly. "I'm going to walk down to the village for some milk."

"Can I come with you?"

Clair almost said no, but seeing the pain in his eyes, the identical pain she felt, she sympathised. "If you want to, but you'll need your walking boots, it's nearly two miles and I like to take the shortcut over the hill. You have an old pair somewhere. I'll find them for you."

Ken followed her through to the kitchen and then on to the utility room where the outdoor clothes were stored.

Clair rooted around in one of the units until she found what she was looking for, and handed the boots to Ken. The leather was dry and stiff and had a mildewy sheen as if they hadn't been worn since the dark ages.

"As you see, you aren't much of a walker, Ken. You'll find some dubbin in that unit over there," she said, pointing to a unit under an old stone sink. He found the tin of dubbin and an old brush.

While he worked on the boots, Clair went out of the room and came back a few minutes later with a brown lambswool jumper which she handed to him. "Here, you'll need this, it's chilly out despite the sun." Ken slipped it over the casual shirt he was wearing, then brushed his hand over his head as if tidying his hair, and was almost surprised when he felt his hair was still like a very short brush.

They left the house and Clair set a quick pace toward a hill a short distance away, her long legs easily eating into the climb. Ken, following behind, found the going hard work at first, and his breath came in short gasps. Then his second wind kicked in and he settled into the rhythm of the pace. Clair was no longer pulling away from him. They reached the top and stood gazing into the valley set out below them. He could see the steeple of the church sticking up through the trees surrounding the village. The view was similar to the one in the watercolour back at the house. He mentioned it to Clair.

"Yes, I did the painting last summer. I love it up here, especially on days like this."

He could understand why. He felt exhilarated, breathed in the April fresh air, his troubles seeming to sail away from him like the puffy white clouds above. He glanced at Clair and she met his eyes with hers. "Thanks," he said, and saw Clair understood his feelings with just that one word.

"We'll leave our troubles here for now," she said solemnly, and led the way to a farm track that snaked its way through some trees and onto the narrow tarmac road leading to the village.

It was one of those quaint country lanes, only wide enough to take a farm tractor, and lined with high embankments topped with spiked hawthorn, and had constant sharp bends with occasional straights. They had been walking the road for ten minutes or so when they passed a Range Rover. It had pulled into a passing place and the dark tinted windows made the interior a shadowy blur. Ken noticed the vehicle had been fitted with larger tyres than normal which gave it an aggressive 'get out of my way' look. Probably belongs to one of those macho drivers who think they own the road, he thought.

They walked on and he could see the road was straight for about the next quarter mile. Ken noticed Clair had the habit of looking over her shoulder every to often to see if any traffic was approaching from behind. He started to do the same. They were about halfway along the straight when he checked over his shoulder and saw the Range Rover pull out from where it had parked and start to race towards them. Ken had the dreadful sense the driver was aiming either to frighten them or run them down. His eyes flicked to the end of the straight, much too far, flicked to the banking on either side and spied a three foot gap in the hawthorn on top. His adrenalin kicked in, a vision of KINSMAN blinked in his mind, and his body took control of his panicking thoughts, blanking them out with a tremendous urge for action. Clair was staring behind seemingly frozen by the sight of the oncoming vehicle. He picked her up, hauled her shoulder high against the banking so she could reach the top and scramble into the gap. He swung back into the middle of the road, The vehicle was driving straight at him.

He ignored Clair's high pitched anguished scream.

He took a deep breath and held it, his eyes focused and concentrated one hundred percent on the monster bearing down on him. The timing would have to be spot on. If he moved too soon the driver would have time to swerve the Range Rover into him. If he moved too late he would be squashed like a bug. He gave the driver the finger, made as if to go left and as the vehicle swerved in that direction he turned, flung himself the opposite way and buried his body and face in the thick coarse grass and other organic life that grew on the hedge. At that precise moment a flock of memories flew through his mind. Dear god! What a time to remember his past! The vehicle swished so close he could feel the slipstream and the touch of the wing mirror as light as a butterfly wing on his back. It all happened in a split second but seemed an eternity.

The adrenaline rush drained away and he collapsed on the roadway, his body trembling and his mouth dry from the near death experience. He watched the vehicle's brake-lights flicker on then off again as the driver corrected the high speed slide and disappeared around a bend in the road. The vehicle registration had been blotted out with mud.

Clair slid down the banking.

He picked himself off the roadway and stood on shaky legs.

Clair threw herself into his arms, nearly knocking him off his feet, hugging him so tight he could hardly breathe. He hugged her back for a few seconds before saying, "It's ok, sweetheart, and I think we'd better get moving in case he decides to return."

"But he's gone. Surely he won't come back?"

"He will if he's determined to kill us. And from the way he drove at me, that was the intention."

Clair nodded her understanding. "Best we go back the way we came then. How are you for running?"

"We'll just have to see, come on."

Clair easily pulled ahead of him in the first hundred yards.

The adrenaline surge had given him the strength to lift Clair high enough to grab for safety, it had given him fast acting wits to foil the murderous driver, but it hadn't given him stamina for a long run back to safety.

Clair slowed when she saw he was struggling and dropped back to keep alongside him for the rest of the way, despite his constant urgings for her to go ahead.

As they headed back to the wood he remembered the real memories from his past that had flashed through his mind. But details of the car accident remained stubbornly blank.

They reached the woods and left the road before stopping and bending over to catch their breath. Clair recovered first.

"I just can't believe you outwitted that monster, darling. I nearly had a heart attack! God, I'm so proud of you. You saved us from certain death."

"I'll be honest with you, sweetheart. I can't believe I've done such a hair-raising thing myself. I had a massive adrenaline rush, and a vision from that dream about KINSMAN and it was as if my body took control over everything else. I think I must be going mad."

"Well, whatever it was, you saved my life. But why would someone want to harm to us?"

"I have a pretty good idea, but I think we should get away from this place first."

"We could go back to the house. And I think we should ring the police, don't you?."

"Later, maybe. But you should hear what I have to say first."

She looked at him puzzled. "Have it your way. Come on I know just the place."

They walked up the track and Clair led him a few yards off it to a gritstone outcrop that formed a seat overlooking the valley. They sat, and Clair said, "Isn't it beautiful?"

"Yes it is. But it could have been "the valley of death.."

Clair shivered. "Don't say that, darling."

"Sorry it just slipped out. Over reaction, probably."

"Forget it. Just tell me what you want to say."

He took a deep breath. "I'm not your husband, sweetheart. My name is Tom Armstrong..."

CHAPTER 10

Clair stared intensely at him, searching his face, her eyes finally locking on to his. Her thoughts racing back over the last few weeks, the dramatic change in Ken's character and the constant nagging doubts in her heart and mind. And she remembered his own serious doubts of being Ken Birkenshaw, her husband. It was like a slot machine, the symbols clicking into place until they all matched. And she was so relieved, and happy.

"Tom Armstrong? And you are not my husband?"

He shook his head. "I'm sorry, Clair."

"Oh, don't be sorry, darling. I'm so relieved. I couldn't understand how you could be so different since the accident. It was doing my head in. I started thinking of you as old Ken and new Ken and hoping you would stay as new Ken when your memory returned. And then last night..." She suddenly leaned over and kissed him passionately on the lips. He held her tight against his chest, prolonging her kiss with equal passion. She pulled away from him, running her fingers over his face. "Tom? Did you say Armstrong? I like it, Armstrong. So much better than Birkenshaw." He laughed. "But you look so like him. Are you twins?

Funny, he never mentioned it."

"No. We are not twins. Well not as far as I know. My mother and father never mentioned a twin brother...unless of course they didn't want me to know. No, my aunt Alice would have told me. I think."

Clair suddenly stood up, frowning as another possible thought hit her; "Remember what Dt Miller said? You may have created a totally different persona. You might still be my husband?"

"I'm absolutely certain I'm Tom Armstrong, Clair. No doubts at all."

"Absolutely Certain?"

"Yes, sweetheart! And I'll tell you another thing. I'm a computer programmer. Not a fancy property developer."

An urgent question came knocking. "Are you married?" Clair held her breath.

"No, sweetheart. And I am not in a relationship either."

Clair let her breath go. "So, next question. What's happened to Ken?"

"It was either him in that vehicle or he's done a runner with all that money."

"Stealing the money? Yes, I could believe that. And I know he can be awful sometimes, but not a murderer, surely?" Then she remembered the look on his face thrust into hers and how frightened she had been. Who knew what he could do?

"You believe it was him in that vehicle, don't you?" Clair said.

"Yes, love."

"Why?"

"Look at the clues, sweetheart. Whoever was in the Range Rover was waiting for us. Right?"

"Could have been waiting for us."

"Ok, could have. But let's assume the driver was waiting for us. How did he...she know we would be on that road at that particular time?"

"You tell me?"

"I think your mobile is bugged. If not that, then your house."

"Bugged? You may have had your memory back, Tom, but now you're being absurd. That's spy story stuff."

"Oh, Clair. No wonder I love you. You're such an innocent at times. Modern listening devices are used by lots of people, even husbands and wives. Easily proved if I'm wrong. Just give me your phone a minute."

Clair reached for her back pocket where she

kept her mobile and handed it to Tom.

He examined it, switched it on, pressed a few buttons and listened. He cancelled the call then did the same routine; pressed a few buttons listened and switched the phone off. "How long have you had it, sweetheart?" he said, handing it back to her.

"Ages. Well, not quite. I've had the same sim card, but Ken gave me the phone over a month ago. Why?"

"It's more than an ordinary mobile. It's a listening device as well. I take it we agree it's now your husband at the bottom of all this intrigue?" Seeing the look on Clair's face, he modified what he was going to say; "If it is him, he could have recorded everything we said while you had the phone near you."

Clair stared at the phone as if it was a viper. "What do you mean everything. Everything we've said to each other since we met?"

"Not only that, love, but every phone call you've made or received on the mobile would have been recorded."

Clair was stunned and then she realised what Tom was implying. "He can hear us talking right at this minute?"

"It was set to record. I've deactivated it and

set it so anyone trying to use it for listening will give their GSM position away. Handy if the police want to pinpoint where the call has come from. Shall I hang on to it for now?"

Clair, grimaced, and it handed back to him. "I never thought Ken would go to such lengths as to spy on me. Iris was right all along - she hates him for what he tried to do to her on my wedding day. She is adamant he tried to have sex with her, and is convinced he is the most deceitful man she'd ever met. She is forever telling me I only see him through rose coloured glasses."

Tom looked at her sympathetically.

"Come on," she said, making an attempt to pull herself together. "Let's go back home."

He stood up, his muscles a bit stiff at first but they soon loosened up as they walked back to the house. He glanced at Clair, her face a picture of despondency and he loathed to remind her of more bad news. "We'll have to check the house for bugs as well, sweetheart."

Tom used the mobile to scan for listening devices after downloading an app. Clair followed him from room to room, watching him get a negative response from the mobile. Tom explained that using the mobile to detect bugs was not a foolproof way of finding listening devices and it would need a scanner to do the job properly. "We can also try searching for them by using our eyes or even our ears, sweetheart. But if your husband has used top of the range devices then they will be difficult to find."

"Oh, let's just forget about them for now. I'll ring Iris and ask if we can stay with her until we sort out what we are going to do. I'll use the land-line, I don't trust that mobile anymore."

"I agree we should get away from this place, especially now we know that your husband tried to kill us, well me anyway."

"Do you think he'd try to kill us here?" Clair said, shocked at the thought.

"Who knows, sweetheart. He must be un-stable to steal all that money and then to attempt murder, not once but twice."

"Right, best get on then!" Tom admired how she was starting to accept Ken Birkenshaw could be such a villain and how he had fooled her since she married him.

Clair was gone for nearly ten minutes before she returned to the kitchen. "I've given Iris a brief explanation of what happened this afternoon and about you, Tom. And why we think it best to stay with her. I could tell she didn't believe half of what I was saying. But she has agreed we can stay with her."

"I don't blame her not believing your husband could have attempted murder."

"Oh, she has no trouble believing Ken could contemplate murder. It's you being Tom Armstrong and not Ken Birkenshaw she finds difficult to swallow. Anyway, I'd better pack a few things; I think you ought to do the same."

Tom agreed and followed Clair upstairs.

Clair's telephone call worried Iris. It seemed absurd to her that Ken Birkenshaw was claiming he was in fact Tom Armstrong, a computer programmer. The story he was identical to that man sounded totally false to her and an obvious scam to escape prosecution for the theft of millions of pounds. Poor Clair she believed the rogue and was prepared to swear he was not her husband. Well he was not going to fool her. She only had to look into his eyes to see the lurking heartless devil behind the mask. Her instinct warned her that Birkenshaw could be dangerous if cornered and she had better arm herself for the confrontation. She went to the dining room, took the ornamental poker from its stand by the fireplace, hefted it to satisfy herself it was 'fit for purpose' and carried it to the umbrella stand which was by the front door.

CHAPTER 11

Clair drove them the ten miles to Baslow where Iris lived. On the journey she explained Iris had gained the house as part of a divorce settlement from her last husband. "James was a jolly nice chap. Too easy going for Iris, I think. He works for an investment bank and Iris being an accountant, it seemed they had a lot in common. But he likes golf and she hates it. Her first husband used golf as a coverup for an affair with his secretary. I will admit she can be hard at times, but generally with a good reason."

"I'll be honest, sweetheart, I'm not looking forward to meeting your sister. What with her hating your husband and divorcing two of her own. Maybe it would be better if I stayed in a hotel."

"Oh, no, Tom Armstrong. You are not getting away from me that easy. Iris is a peach when you get to know her. But she has always looked out for me and can be over protective sometimes. Anyway, you've got no money, have you?"

"Christ, I'll have to check my online bank accounts, and hope he hasn't been able to access them. I wonder if your sister has a computer at home?"

"Yes she has. And I'm sure she'll lend it to you if only to gain proof you are who you say you are."

Tom noticed the impressive gateway flanked by ornate pillars, each topped with a concrete pineapple as Clair drove through and up a short drive to park outside the front door. The house was double fronted and Clair had already told him it had five bedrooms, all en suite.

Clair tried the door handle but found it locked and she pressed the bell.

A short wait and then the door was opened by Iris, who ushered them into a brightly lit hallway and then re-locked and bolted the door behind them. Tom couldn't take his eyes from the brass handled poker Iris held down by her side. It looked as if it could cleave the head of a wildebeest.

Clair introduced Tom and he held out his hand. "Pleased to meet you, Iris."

Iris ignored the hand and the greeting. She placed herself in front of him but a good yard away and because of her smaller stature she had to look up at his face. Her mouth was drawn into a thin line, and her jaw jutted aggressively forward. She held the poker off the floor and pointing slightly forward. To Tom it looked ready for action. He raised his eyes from the poker and found Iris staring at him with hazel eyes that were like chips of ice. He became worried at how long he could gaze into those cold eyes before he was turned to stone. The hazel seemed to change colour with all the anger and hate dancing in their depths. Then they softened, the hazel brightened, her jaw relaxed and her mouth took on its natural fullness. She turned away from him and spoke to Clair, who had been watching the exchange.

"He's not bloody Birkenshaw, love. He hasn't got a deceitful shifty look in the back of his eyes that your husband tries to hide with a charmer's smile. But you are right, he looks exactly like Ken Birkenshaw to pass for him."

Tom glanced at Clair and tried a tentative smile. Clair's smile was more full, she trusted Iris's instinct and was happy Tom had passed her sister's examination..

Iris led the way along the hall and placed the poker by the dining room door before moving on to the lounge which was furnished with a pale green three seater settee facing a marble fireplace and two armchairs placed either side of it. A long low coffee table was arranged between the soft furnishings. Iris motioned Clair and Tom to the settee while she sat in one of the armchairs. Then she gave Tom a penetrating stare, and tapped the end of her upturned nose with her index finger. "You may not be Clair's husband but I see his hand manipulating all this deceit. What I want to know is if you and he are partners?"

"No, I'm not involved with him, I assure you. In fact I don't even know the man and I've given Clair an outline of what I can remember before the car accident but I'm not able to remember the accident itself. And since then, it's been a roller coaster of events that's hardly given Clair or me a chance to analyse what is happening to us."

"And you don't think you are his twin?"

"Not to my knowledge."

"Well, to be exactly like Birkenshaw, I'd bet my life you are his twin brother. You are two siblings out of the same egg. No other way."

Tom shrugged. "I'll not argue. But I was never told I had a twin by my parents or my mother's sister, aunt Alice."

"Clair mentioned your parents are dead. Killed in a plane crash. How old were you when they died?"

"Eleven, going on twelve."

"It's possible the knowledge was kept from you until you were old enough to understand the breakup. Social Services would be loathe to separate twins, especially identical twins because of their close affinity to each other. Have you ever felt something missing from your life?"

"No not really, except for losing my mother

and father. It was such a shock when they died so suddenly it did cause me some mental pain."

"Do you know where you were born?"

"Nottingham. According to my birth certificate."

"Right. And where do you live now?"

"London mostly. I was booked into a B&B and I've been working with another programmer on a video game. He has a family and lives in Sheffield. We'd just finished ironing out the problems in a video program as a matter of fact and I was intending to move back to London."

Clair butted in to their conversation. "Can we just accept Tom is genuine, and inform the police. I really think they should investigate the car accident and the attempted murder this afternoon."

"There is a problem we have to take into account, love," Tom said. "You're forgetting Richard Cartwright. I don't think he'd want the loss of such a large amount of money made public if there's a good chance the money can be recovered. And if the police became involved at this stage you can guarantee the news media would soon sniff out the scandal."

"I agree," Iris said. "But for a different reason. We have to have cast iron proof this guy, here, is in fact Tom Armstrong and how he became involved with Ken Birkenshaw. Otherwise, in my opinion, the police are not going to bother to investigate."

"Well, Tom can give you proof of who he is. He'd like to borrow your computer to see if his bank accounts are still secure."

Iris looked at Tom with a raised eyebrow. "Because you think Ken Birkenshaw has not only double crossed you, but taken your money as well?"

"I wish you'd stop inferring Tom is involved with Ken, Iris," Clair said, before Tom could answer. "He's already told you he wasn't."

"Alright! Alright! Have it your way. I'll get the laptop." She abruptly left the room.

Clair smiled at Tom and shrugged her shoulders.

Iris returned with her laptop and sat in her armchair. She opened up the machine, switched it on and quickly entered her password. She waited until the desktop image was showing then handed the computer to Tom.

His fingers raced over the keys as he accessed his online banking. A half minute later he was in and searching through his accounts. He looked up, first at Clair and then at Iris. "There's a few hundred pounds taken from my current account. All in small amounts. I suppose your husband or

Mandy have been using my contactless debit card. But the other accounts have not been tampered with and they are still secure. You can see the accounts if you wish, proof I'm Tom Armstrong."

"I don't want to see them," Clair said. "I trust you implicitly."

Iris reached for the computer. "Do you mind?"

Tom handed it across.

It only took a few seconds for Iris to satisfy herself and then she handed the machine back to Tom for him to exit his online bank accounts. Tom placed the computer on the coffee table when he'd finished.

Iris picked up the computer and said, "I'll go and make us something to drink. "Tea, coffee or something stronger?"

"Coffee, will be fine," Clair said.

"Same, here," Tom said

When Iris had left the room, Clair whispered: "That was Iris's way of apologising for doubting you, darling."

"I'm pleased we've finally convinced her."

Clair rose and said, "I'll go and see if she wants a hand."

A few minutes later Clair was back carrying a tray on which were coffee cups and some plates and a box of chocolate biscuits. She set out the plates and coffee cups and opened the box of biscuits. By the time she'd finished Iris walked in with the coffee. Iris busied herself with serving them the coffee and encouraging them to select the biscuits. And when that was done and she was seated again, she said. "Alright, Tom, do you mind if I ask you some questions regarding your background?"

"Ask away."

"Have you ever met Ken Birkenshaw"?

"Not to my knowledge."

"Let's just come back to the car accident."

"That's a memory I just can't recall, no matter how hard I try. The hospital found traces of Ketamine and alcohol in my blood and I assume I was drugged by Ken Birkenshaw."

"I thought you hadn't met Ken, so how could he have given you those drugs?"

"I can't remember meeting him. But I have met a very close friend of his by the name of Mandy Sitwell. Do you know her?"

"She's a secretary or PA or something like that to Richard Arkwright." Clair butted in. "I've only met her a couple of times - thought she was a bit of a man eater...." Clair saw a blush starting on Tom's face. "Have you had a relationship with her, Tom

Armstrong."

"You could say that, sweetheart. But I hadn't met you then and I already suspected she was having an affair with someone else."

"With my husband, I bet!"

"I honestly don't know, love. She was fun to be with at first. But then she started squirrelling away at my personal details and I caught her once trying to access my computer. And I began to realise she was acting a part. She did in fact say she belonged to an amateur theatrical society. So I just had the thought when we were coming here that she was trying to gather information for your husband to use. May be a wild guess."

"You could have taken the drugs yourself," Iris said. "And been driving the car of your own accord."

"I can't drive, and I don't do drugs. And I'm a moderate drinker."

"You can't drive!" Clair and Iris said in unison. And then they laughed.

Tom looked at them, puzzled. "What's so funny?"

"Tom Armstrong," Clair said, "don't you realise you are a rarity in this part of the world. Nearly everyone in our age group who can afford a car has one."

"Well, living in London and owning a car can be a pain. Parking, congestion charges, car insurance, tax, etc., when public transport or a taxi is cheaper and stress free in the end."

"OK. Point taken." Iris said. "In actual fact, you being in the car alone and not being able to drive could be enough for the police to investigate a possible murder attempt. We just tell Richard Cartwright that is what we are going to do, seeing how Ken Birkenshaw has decided murder is on the cards."

"Do you think Cartwright will believe Tom is not Ken? He didn't this morning."

"That won't be difficult, love. And I've had business dealing with that rogue in the past. He and Birkenshaw have the same money mentality - anything goes providing there's a profit at the end. I'll give him a ring now and ask for a meeting. Best face to face, I think." She he rose and walked over to a small table and picked up the telephone. She consulted a note book that was by the side of the phone and dialled a number. She listened and then said, "Blast!" And left a message saying who she was and would like to speak to him urgently. She put the phone down and came back to her armchair. "He's not in, I've left a message on his answer machine." She looked at the clock on the mantlepiece. Six-fifteen. "I'll start to prepare an evening meal. If he hasn't rung back by the time we finish the meal I'll give him another ring and impress on him how urgent it is."

They had just finished their meal when there was a bleep from the cctv Iris had placed on the drinks cabinet. It showed Mandy Sitwell and a bearded man standing at the front door. Then the doorbell rang.

"Who are they?" Iris said.

"That's Mandy Sitwell." Tom said, "Don't recognise the bloke with her though."

"Neither do I. Wonder what they want," Clair said.

"Better find out, I suppose," Iris said, rising out of he chair.

Tom, who was sitting nearest the dining room door said, "I'll go, if you like?"

"Just be careful, Tom." Iris said, and moved towards the fireplace to pick up the poker with the ornamental brass handle.

Tom walked down the hallway and opened the door.

PART TWO

Back to when Mandy met Tom for the first time.

CHAPTER 12

Mandy was not in a good mood. She was late for her lunch booking and her friend had cancelled at the last moment. She was about to push open the restaurant door when it was opened from within by the spitting image of Ken Birkenshaw. "Ken! What the hell are you doing here!" she said, before realising he couldn't be Ken because he'd gone to Manchester with Richard Cartwright, her boss.

"I think you've mistaken me for someone else." The man said.

She studied him for a few seconds, amazed how he looked like Ken. Same blonde hair, cut shorter but with the same curl. Those lovely blue eyes, and the straight nose above a hint of a smile.

"Sorry, love. But you are very similar to a friend of mine." Her mind was racing and she wanted to know more about him. "You are leaving? Did you enjoy your meal?"

"No," he said, "This place was recommended but apparently you have to book." He was obviously irritated.

"Well, they do have a good reputation." A glimmer of an idea forming. "Tell you what. I was supposed to be having lunch with a friend, but she's cancelled. Why don't you have lunch with me," she said, giving him her most enticing smile.

She saw him hesitating. So she stuck out her hand. "Mandy Sitwell, and you are?"

He grinned at her, exactly like Ken's grin. "Tom Armstrong," he said taking her hand in his. "I'll take you up on your offer, Mandy, providing you'll let me pay."

"Off course," she laughed. "That's what gentlemen are for."

He held the door open for her and then followed her in.

The interior was done out in mock Victorian decor; sepia photographs of Sheffield around the late 19th to early 20th century and fake gas lamps against red flock wallpaper. The tables were dotted throughout the room, and covered with check tablecloths. Nearly all the tables were occupied, and those that were not had a 'Reserved' notice on them.

The head waiter knew Mandy, and she motioned to Tom saying, "He's with me, Henry."

"Very good Miss Sitwell." He waited until

they had removed their overcoats and Tom had hung them on nearby hooks, before showing them to her favourite table by the window. He handed them a menu each and moved back to his position by the door.

She couldn't help studying Tom as he was so much like Ken, it was hard for her not to start treating him as she would her lover. He even looked about thirty, the same age. "Do you have a twin brother, Tom?"

"No. I don't have any siblings."

Mandy decided to drop it for now. "Do you live in Sheffield?"

"Just temporary. I'm a computer programmer, and I've come up from London to work with a Sheffield chap over next few weeks or so."

"So where are you staying?"

"I'm booked into a B&B. Not far from here, actually.'

Mandy nodded and turned her attention to the menu. "What are you going to have?" she said.

"The sirloin, I think. And you?"

"The same," she said, placing the menu on the table. "New potatoes with all the trimmings. And what about some wine, any particular favourite?"

"A good merlot?"

"Ok, Tom. Let's settle for that."

Tom glanced around, trying to find a waiter. There was one walking purposefully towards their table. Mandy said before he arrived, "I'm a regular here. And a good tip provides good service."

The waiter smiled at Mandy first and then at Tom before taking their orders. When he had gone, Mandy said, "So, Tom, do you know Sheffield?"

"Not really. Jeff, the programmer I'm working with is married and has a young daughter so I've been left to explore on my own. Not really an exciting experience."

Perfect. She puffed out her full red lips, arched an eyebrow and let her cool grey eyes linger on his. At twenty-nine she knew she had a figure that could easily entice young and old studs into bed and she had cultivated the sexual foreplay that rarely failed her. Much of which she had practiced on her actor friends in the Amateur Theatre Group she belonged to.

A wine waiter arrived with the house merlot. Tom indicated Mandy should taste it.. Mandy pronounced it satisfactory and let Tom fill their glasses.

Then she continued gathering information.

"Where do you live in London?"

"I have a studio flat in Chiswick. Been there a few years now. But I'm originally from Nottingham."

"Must be expensive keeping a car in London, what with the congestion charge and I suppose garaging if the price of houses are any yardstick?"

"I don't have a car," Tom said. "Don't have a driving licence, even."

"You do surprise me, young Tom. No driving licence. How do you prove who you are?"

"Oh, I have passport and if more is needed I can supply a birth certificate. Why? You are not asking for my hand in marriage, are you, Mandy?" Tom, smiled at her and she noticed how the corners of his eyes crinkled just like Ken's.

"Not yet, Tom Armstrong. Maybe the next leap year. Are you in a relationship?"

He smiled and shook his head. "Been there a few times, but free at the moment. What about yourself?"

Mandy decided to tell an outright lie. "Same as you, Tom. They come and go." She laughed, showing her perfect white teeth.

They continued to exchange information until their meal arrived.

Mandy told Tom she was Sheffield born and bred and was a secretary to a Richard Cartwright, investor and property developer.

"Ken Birkenshaw, who could be your twin, is a friend and sometimes partner in property developing with Richard."

When they were finished, they declined the desert and just ordered coffee. Mandy asked if Tom had enjoyed the meal.

"Couldn't have been better, Mandy. Do you have to go back to work?"

"Yes, I'm afraid so. But no rush. Richard is at a meeting in Manchester."

Mandy easily read Tom's disappointment. And thought, now to reel you in. "But I'm free this evening if you would like me to show you some Sheffield night life?"

"Oh, thanks. I'm not putting you out, am I?"

"I wouldn't have offered if you were, Tom. Give me you address and I'll pick you up at seventhirty."

Tom give her the address which she wrote in a small note book she took from her handbag. She leaned over to write and he admired the way her blonde hair was permed into soft curls, and he wondered why a sexy looking woman like Mandy seemed eager to make a date with him.

They also exchanged phone numbers before parting.

Later in the evening, before going to collect Tom Armstrong, Mandy rang Ken.

He wasn't too happy to get the call because he was in the middle of dressing to take some clients out for an evening meal. "What is it, Mandy?" he said into his mobile.

"We need to meet, darling. I met your twin this afternoon and I think he's the answer to that problem we discussed last weekend."

"What the hell are you talking about? I don't have a twin."

"Put it this way, Tom Armstrong could be taken for you in bright sunlight. Same build, same facial features, if you saw him you could be looking in a mirror. I've made a date with him for this evening to keep him interested. But like I said, we need to meet urgently to make some plans. Are you going to be in the office tomorrow? Or are you staying over in Manchester?"

Mandy listened to the silence and knew Ken was thinking about her information.

"Alright, sexpot. I wasn't intending to come in, but if you think it's that urgent I'll see you tomorrow. I Know Richard won't be in and we'll be able to have a good chat then."

"Right. See you then, lover-boy."

Mandy took Tom to a disco where live music was played by a local boy band. Thursday night and the place was packed with a young crowd, determined to dance themselves to exhaustion. Mandy and Tom sat at one of the small tables on upper balcony where they could look down at the heaving bodies. Tom had a pint of larger and Mandy sipped a Blue Hawaiian. She had dressed with care, tight fitting little black dress, low cut to show off her deep cleavage and mid thigh to show off her toned legs. Her honey blonde curls were loose to her shoulders and glinted in the disco lights. She had used her most expensive seductive perfume. She was a sex machine waiting to engage.

Tom had dressed casually, black t-shirt with black trousers.

When the band played and the crowd danced and shrieked there was no way they could converse without their faces almost touching. On those occasions when Mandy leaned in close to say something, Tom's libido whirled and his testosterone danced in the aura of her perfume and the vision of her cleavage. When she suggested they hit the dance floor he hoped the energy he expended on the dance floor would bring some relief. But Mandy used dance to keep him hyped. She wiggled, shimmied, and threw her body into such convoluted twists and turns that Tom and a good portion of the dancers around them wondered how she kept her dress on and her marvellous breasts from flying out.

It took nearly an hour of exuberant dances before he was able to coax Mandy off the floor, and back to a seat where he could try to cool down.

"God! I enjoyed that!" Mandy said, laughing as they found seats in the lounge, off from the dance floor. "Hold my seat for me, will you, love. I have to use the loo."

"Drink?" He asked, before she moved off.

"Better make it tonic with lemon, please. I'm driving."

Mandy was gone fifteen minutes before she returned looking as fresh as when she had picked Tom up from the B&B. He marvelled at her recovery process.

She sat down, gave him a pouty smile, thinking although he might look identical to Ken, how different they were in character. Ken was more brash, more of a party animal, just like her. Tom seemed more the quiet type, more of a listener. She picked up her drink, and gave him a smile over the rim before taking a sip. "Needed that," she said putting the glass back on the table. "How about you, Tom. Have you enjoyed the evening?"

"Great, thanks, Mandy," he said, holding his pint glass up to salute her. "Though I think another dance and I would have collapsed on that floor. I don't know where you get all that energy from."

"The secret is working out three time a week, love." Mandy said, chuckling. "And I do love dancing. Keeps a girl's figure in trim." She give him a coy look and smoothed her hand down the front of her dress. She saw Tom's eyes follow her hand down to her lower tummy.

"You are certainly a good advert for that, young lady" he said with a grin.

When they finished their drinks. Mandy suggested they leave. They had to wait for their overcoats in the foyer while the checkout girl found them. Mandy leaned in close to Tom's arm and did a little shiver. "Bit cold out here," she said. Tom automatically put his arm around her waist and pulled her in against him.

"Um." She reached up and gave him a peck on the cheek.

Their coats arrived and they left the building to hurry across the carpark to Mandy's KIA, SUV. She quickly switched on the engine, waited a few seconds for Tom to put his seatbelt on, put the car in gear and drove out of the carpark. The disco was the other side of Sheffield to the B&B and they were quiet on the drive back, with Mandy concentrating on her driving, and Tom almost asleep after the hectic evening and the drinks. She pulled up outside the B&B but didn't shut off the engine. They turned towards each other. Mandy pursed her rose red lips inviting a kiss. Tom obliged, but when he started to to take it further Mandy gently pushed him back. "I think we should leave it there for now, Tom Armstrong. We're both tired and if you enjoyed my company we can alway's make another date."

Tom was disappointed but she was right. He was almost bone tired. So he worked up a smile. "Of course I enjoy your company, young lady."

"How about next Monday? "I'll take you somewhere quieter. Do you like the theatre?"

"Depends on the show. I like a good drama or a musical or even a good comedy."

Mandy laughed. "Well I'm sure I'll be able to come up with something out of that lot." She placed her lips on Tom's for a quick kiss and said, "Off you go then. See you Monday about seven."

On the drive back to her flat she congratulated herself for a job well done.

CHAPTER 13

Ken had recently closed his own office when Richard had offered him use of an empty suite of offices in his building. It had suited Ken business wise (he and Richard often partnered in property development projects) and also because he and Mandy had started a relationship. Ken had brought one of his office girls to act as secretary and made the other two redundant at the suggestion of Richard telling Ken could use his staff if he wished. Ken wasn't fooled by Richard's generosity. He knew Richard wanted to keep him close to benefit from Ken's contacts and great selling skills. But if Ken and Mandy's plans came to fruition Richard would rue the day he had invited Ken into his domain.

On Friday morning Ken and Mandy sat in his office discussing her proposed plan.

"It's like I said, darling, Mandy emphasised. "Tom Armstrong could be your identical twin brother and if we plan it right he could be our fall guy, as they say in gangster movies."

"And how do you propose we do that."

"I haven't thought too deeply about it, I wanted to discuss it with you first. But you know, how we were puzzling which way to steal the money and not be on the run from the police or

Richard. Well, we need to figure out a way for Armstrong to take the blame, and for you to take his identity."

"I'd like to see this Tom Armstrong for myself before we go any further."

Mandy was miffed Ken hadn't taken her word about Tom being identical. But she knew when Ken said he wanted to see Tom for himself it was pointless to argue with him. "That will be easy But you should be careful you are not seen together by anyone else. They could be a witness against us in the future." She thought for a second and then said. "What about if you sit in your car near where he is staying and see what you think when he leaves."

Ken gave a cautious nod. Then said, "What about the disguise we tried out. I could even fool Clair, don't you think?."

"Oh, Ken, it was only a last resort. And you'd have to dye your hair and wear a false beard until you grew your own."

Ken stared at her, assessing her advice. Finally, he said, "Ok, you set it up and I'll watch from the car."

"I'm seeing him on Monday but it will be dark then. What if I ring him and see if he's free either Saturday afternoon or Sunday afternoon. I can suggest a run out in the car and a stop at a pub or something."

"Saturday is out, but Sunday will be fine."

Mandy rang Tom and when she got through she asked if he'd like to take a run out in the car with her on Sunday afternoon. Tom said he'd be delighted. She suggested two in the afternoon.

"He's agreed," she said putting her mobile away in a pocket of her jeans.

Ken had been quietly thinking about how to use this Tom Armstrong if he was identical to himself. And he concluded murder would have to be done. Strangely it did not bother him one iota. After all, he'd done it once before and got clean away with it. All it needed was opportunity.

Sunday afternoon, just before 2pm, Ken parked his car a couple of doors down from the B&B where Tom Armstrong was staying. It was a oneway street and too narrow for permanent parking. Mandy had already told him provided he didn't park too long there would be no problem. Mandy arrived shortly thereafter and gave Ken an unobtrusive wave as she drove past his car and parked outside of the B&B. Armstrong must have been waiting for her because he opened the door almost immediately and strolled to the passenger side of Mandy's car. Mandy pretended not to have unlocked the car doors and left Armstrong to fiddle with the door handle for several seconds until she pressed the release button for him to get in. It was sufficient time for Ken to study Armstrong. And like Mandy, he was amazed Tom Armstrong was identical to him. Time to start some serious planning.

He waited until Mandy's car had disappeared before starting his car and heading back home. While he drove he mulled over the problem of murder and how to get away with it. The best bet, he thought, was for it to look like an accident. Pity Armstrong didn't use drugs. An overdose, just like his mother and stepfather would be ideal. He smiled to himself at that one. A suicide? A car accident? All possibles. But it would need a lot more thought. And Mandy would have to be on board, and he would make sure she had a hand in it, otherwise she would be a threat.

His money worries had started four months previously when a star rated company he had invested nearly all his money in had gone bankrupt. All he had left was about ten thousand which was disappearing at an alarming rate just to cover his present lifestyle. A disaster he had kept strictly to himself. Not even Mandy knew about it The stress of deceiving Richard and the rest of the investors was affecting his nerves and he was having trouble sleeping. He was also having trouble keeping his temper with Clair. He had never really been in love with her. Thought he would be able to get the land she owned and put some expensive properties on it. Her father had put the knife into that project by making sure Clair wouldn't be persuaded to sign half over to him.

Come to that, he'd never really been in love with anyone. He enjoyed Mandy's company and she was great in bed. She had also been of tremendous help in acquiring the passwords and Richard's personal details. But love never entered into their relationship as far as he was concerned. His thoughts returned to Tom Armstrong and how to set him up to take the blame. The timing would have to be right. He had already considered how to steal the deposits for the latest property development project. There was five million pencilled in against his name - a sum he had no hope of raising. But he had convinced Richard he would have it by the time the money was needed. The deposits from all the investors were held in a joint business account, that could be accessed on line and only needed their passwords and a card reader. The account could be accessed individually for queries but when large funds were needed to be transferred both their passwords were required. Mandy, as Richard's secretary had acquired his password to the bank account. And Richard was in the habit of leaving his laptop on his desk when taking clients for an extended lunch.

The deposit account now held fifty-three million pounds, a sum Ken and Mandy thought they could put to good use if a way could be found of taking the money without being caught. Their latest plan had been to acquire new identities and live abroad. Mandy had mused it would be easy for her to change her appearance and she would help Ken to change his by using her makeup skills. He would have to dye his hair and probably grow a beard. But with Tom Armstrong walking innocently into their devious world, he could be the answer to their dreams.

He rang Mandy Sunday evening and agreed Tom Armstrong was perfect. "Put your thinking cap on, Mandy and we'll discuss how on Wednesday evening at your place, usual time. Oh, and we'd better make sure we are more discreet from now on."

"Of course, handsome," she said, laughing. "I love acting, as you know."

CHAPTER 14

On Monday evening Mandy collected Tom and took him to a small theatre which was putting on a version of 'The King's Speech'.

She left her little black dress in her wardrobe and favoured an almost transparent white blouse and a short black skirt. Tom was dressed in a casual blue shirt and beige trousers and a lightweight jacket. They had a drink in the small bar afterwards and Mandy said, "I was disappointed with the play, thought it was a bit amateurish and the director didn't capture the drama."

"Yes. I thought the film was much better. But then it had top class actors and a director who knew his business. Anyway, it was a nice thought and I'm enjoying the company."

"Why, thank you Tom Armstrong. What about going back to my place after we finish this. I don't like to drink and drive." Mandy had ordered a tonic water with a squeeze of lemon.

Tom was drinking his usual pint. "Why not," he said, giving her a cheeky grin.

Mandy had a one bedroom ground floor flat in a recently built luxury tower block. It had been one of Ken's development projects. She had furnished it with two low black leather sofas, an antique rocking chair, a matching beechwood bookcase, drinks cabinet and a coffee table. It had underfloor heating and inset ceiling lamps which could be dimmed with voice control. Her kitchen was stainless steel and black marble, with enough space to take a small kitchen table and two hard-back chairs.

She motioned Tom to a seat. "What would you like, coffee or something stronger?" she asked after dispensing their overcoats to the hall cupboard.

"Do you have whisky?"

"Certainly." She nearly added, 'It's what Ken drinks'. She would have to be careful. They looked so alike, she could get confused.

Before preparing the drinks, she picked up a remote control from the top of the drinks cabinet, pressed a few buttons to fill the room with some background classical music, She prepared a large measure of whisky for Tom and a small one for herself, adding water to hers. "Do you want water, Tom"

"No, thanks."

Another Ken trait.

She brought the drinks over to the table in front of Tom and sat next to him. He picked up his drink and touched his glass to hers. "Happy hunting," she said, giving him her most seductive smile.

"How are you getting on with the video game, darling?" She wanted to know because he had told her previously he would be going back to London when his programming finished and the game was ready for distribution.

"Friday of this week, I think. We are taking less time than we thought."

"Ah, then we'll have a leaving party," she said. She gave him an arch look, leaned towards him and gave him a lingering kiss on the lips. "Bit of practice needed, don't you think?"

"Plenty of practice, would be the way to go." Tom said, and pulled her into his arms. And for a few minutes they practised, with improvement and passion gaining ground.

Mandy pulled away to take a sip from her glass. Tom followed her example. Then it was back to practicing until Mandy started undoing his shirt buttons while he struggled with her blouse. Mandy suggested they adjourn to the bedroom, where Tom found she favoured a king-size bed and pink silk sheets.

Tom was then pulled into Mandy's lovemaking she had developed into an art form, leaving him an exhausted wreck. Mandy knew she had him hooked.

The following morning she told him she would not be free until Friday and suggested he stay with her Friday night if he had he finished his programming work by then.

"I'll do my best," Tom said, thinking one more night with Mandy would be a good send off from Sheffield.

Mandy was pleased - it would give her an opportunity to access Tom's computer and hopefully his bank account. She had already found out he did his banking online by pretending she was thinking of using the internet, but was worried about the security. He had told her as long as she followed the bank's rules she would be covered by their guarantee. She already knew all this because she actually did her banking online.

They both left the flat together and then went their separate ways for work.

CHAPTER 15

Ken arrived at Mandy's at 6 pm on Wednesday evening, having rung Clair to tell her he would be working late at the office.

They sat at the kitchen table to discuss how they would use Tom Armstrong's identity after the theft of the money.

Mandy mentioned she'd invited Tom to stay with her Friday on night which should give her the opportunity to access his computer and bank accounts. "I thought we could use that Ketamine you have, darling. Doesn't it make victims do what you ask?"

"It can be used as a date rape drug, But the dose has to be fairly accurate. I don't think it can be used as a truth drug, if that's what you have in mind. But while it would be nice to have access to his bank accounts all I'll need is his passport and a birth certificate. Anyway, we'll leave that for the minute." he said, staring into her eyes. "You know we will have to kill him, don't you?"

"I know, darling. And I've been thinking about it since I first met him. And I can't see any other way. But could you make it quick? I don't like to think of him suffering."

Ken's lip curled into a sneer. "You're not falling for him, are you, lover-bean?"

"Of course not! He may be your identical twin, but he's not a patch on you in bed. Bit old fashion actually. Likes to think a woman has to be coaxed into the mood for sex."

"He had a surprise with you then." Ken said, irritated at the thought of Armstrong making love to Mandy.

"Let's move on, shall we," Mandy said, cooly.

"I've thought of all the ways we could dispense with Armstrong. I could make it look like suicide or a mugging. Or an overdose of drugs, always a good one. A car accident maybe. I could go on, but there's one big problem. I've checked and found even if we were identical twins, our finger prints would be different. And mine are on police files from when I was a teenager and was caught stealing. I don't know about Armstrong's."

"Oh, Ken. You never told me. What was it?"

He hesitated then decided to tell a version of the truth his defence lawyer had presented to the court. "A gold watch for a girlfriend I had at the time."

Mandy smiled at him. "And there was I saying Armstrong was old-fashioned. You have hidden depths Ken Birkenshaw."

He shrugged. "What I'm getting at is if he dies

in suspicious circumstances he will likely be fin-gerprinted. Something we cannot take a chance on."

"Right, glad you brought that up. So how do we get round it. Kill him and bury the body?" Mandy grimaced at the thought.

"We could do that, but what if his body is found? No, I think we have a body where the fin-gerprints have been destroyed and the police have a body they will have to assume is mine."

"I thought the reason we were killing Tom Armstrong was that he looked identical to you, darling."

"You are right. And I will still use his identity. But now I've found out he's not as identical as you thought, we will have to modify our plans to get round the problem."

"Well it's starting to get rather complicated, Ken. Maybe we should abandon the whole thing."

Ken's features hardened and he stared at Mandy with ice blue eyes. He quickly reached across the table and clamped her slim wrist with an iron grip. "Don't you even think of abandoning our little project, Sitwell."

"Please, Ken." Mandy had tears forming and tried to pull her hand free. "You're hurting me."

Ken eased his grip but still held onto her

wrist. "Do you understand. We are going to kill that nerd and I'm going to use his identity. And if you are not on board, tell me now."

Mandy was frightened by the look in his eyes and his cold, calculating tone. For the first time she realised there was no way of changing her mind about murder. "Yes, darling. I understand what you are saying. Could you please let my wrist go? It's hurting."

Ken released her wrist and smiled, but it didn't thaw the ice in his eyes. "Right, let's crack on. Like I was saying. We kill Armstrong and make sure his fingerprints are destroyed as well."

"And how do we do that." Mandy couldn't help sulking. She had a strong feeling he had already decided how he would kill Armstrong.

"A car accident where the car will catch fire. Cars are notorious for bursting into flames that not only destroy the car but anyone in it as well."

"Do you have a place in mind."

"Snake Pass. I drove over there and had a scout around. Last month's snow has cleared after the thaw and the heavy rain has caused a landslip. Great for us because there are some flimsy warning barriers where the subsidence has left a gap in the wall. I parked the car and had a look. There's a sheer drop into the ravine. Couldn't be a better place for a car accident. The ravine is not deep.

More of a gully. So we will have to make sure the car will catch fire with Armstrong in it."

"You worked it all out by yourself, Ken. Why didn't you tell me sooner?"

"Only worked it out last night, lover-bird. So what do you think. See any snags?"

"One obviously. How do we get the car to crash through the barrier."

"The hill is steep. We'll just put the car in neutral, start the car and release the hand brake. If it doesn't move we'll give it a push with your car."

"What if another vehicle comes along?"

"Not much traffic uses the Snake these days after dark and, at this time of the year, even less. But if any do come along, we'll see their headlights in plenty of time and just wait until the road is clear."

"When?"

"Friday night. Richard will be away from the office next week, as you well know. So I thought I'd transfer fifty-two million to the Caymans Friday afternoon after Richard leaves. You take care to have Armstrong drugged with the Ketamine. We'll transport him in my car and you will follow in yours."

"I thought you said there was fifty-three million," Mandy said, remembering quite clearly the amount Ken had mentioned to bring her on board.

"Correct. But leaving a mill. will not only keep the account open, it should stop the bank sending a closure notification to Richard."

"What about Armstrong's bank details? And you taking over his identity?"

"All in good time, Mandy, girl. And I'll let you figure out a way to access his computer. But like I said, I'm more interested in a passport and birth certificate. Did you say they were at his flat in London?"

"Yes, and he always carries his keys with him."

"Right, so make sure you have him drugged by the time I arrive."

'I'll do my best, darling."

"Oh, do more than your best, Mandy. I'm relying on you. So earn your keep."

Mandy could see his anger was still simmering. And she knew she'd have to be careful not to give him cause to distrust her. "Shall I make us a drink and a snack or something?"

"Good thinking. But no alcohol. Coffee to keep my head clear."

She made the coffee and made some sandwiches. She knew it would give Ken time to cool off. He was not one to stay angry for long, provided he got his way.

They spent the rest of the evening finalising their plans for Friday night and where he would hide out until they knew everything had gone according to plan.

CHAPTER 16

Tom had roughed out his idea for a video game with a computer program before contacting Jeff Wellmore, a friend from university, who was a genius at virtual programming. They had been working on the programs by using their computers to communicate, but they had run into a difficult problem that would be better solved working together on the same computer.

Jeff was a broad shouldered man with wiry hair and a dark beard. He had invited Tom up to Sheffield, saying it would be impossible for him to travel to London because of family commitments. He apologised for not having a spare bedroom for Tom to stay, but could book him into a good B&B which was within walking distance from where he lived.

Jeff had a three bedroom semi-detached house and lived with his wife Emma and their ten year old daughter, Kim. He had converted the small box room into a computer workshop with two powerful desktop computers attached to thirty-two inch monitors. He also had a laptop, but rarely used it when working on a video game. The room was so small that when he and Jeff were in it, working side by side, there was only enough space to allow a two inch gap between them. But they had good chemistry for working together and by Thursday they had cracked the problem. They spent Friday testing and retesting until they were absolutely confident the video game was ready to send to their distributor, another long-term friend. Tom, watching his hero dispensing with villains right left and centre couldn't help being proud of their achievement. He had been living with 'KINSMAN' inside his head for nearly two years, first as a budding idea, then the continuous programming problems and now a virtual reality. They did the high five gesture several times and couldn't stop grinning at each other.

Emma, at five-foot-eight had the perfect figure and loved wearing tight clothes to show off her curves, but her cool demure stopped males from becoming over friendly. She invited Tom to evening dinner with them seeing as it was his last day, but he declined, apologising, saying he had a date with Mandy.

"Ah," Jeff, said winking at his wife, "We can't interfere with his romantic plans, now can we?"

Tom rang Mandy to say he and Jeff had finished the video and he would be ready whenever she wanted to collect him. Mandy said she finished work at 5pm and would call for him shortly after that.

When Mandy knocked on the door, Mrs

Hoskins, the landlady, answered. She was middle aged and her grey hair was recently permed. She had a motherly face.

"He'll be down in a minute, love."

"Thank you. Mrs Hoskins, isn't it?" Mandy said, remembering Tom had mentioned her name.

"That's right, love. I'll be sorry to see Tom go. He's been a real gentleman."

Mandy heard Tom clattering down the stairs. "Nice to meet you Mrs Hoskins," she said and turned to go back to her car.

"You take good care of him, now, Miss."

"Oh, I will," Mandy said, with a straight face. Then Tom appeared behind Mrs Hoskins and she walked quickly back to her car to open the boot.

Tom emerged carrying a luggage case and a computer shoulder bag. "Bye, Mrs Hoskins, he said, cheerily, giving her a quick kiss on the cheek.

"Bye, Tom. I've told your young lady to take good care of you."

When Tom had put his luggage away and settled himself beside Mandy she said, "Mrs Hoskins seems to have taken to you."

"She's a good sort and a good cook and I've enjoyed staying. Do you know she even cried when I told her I was leaving today?. Would have thought she got used to people coming and going, wouldn't you. Can never tell with folk, these days." He smiled across at her.

Mandy shook her head, put the car in gear and drove off, thinking of what Ken and she had planned for him. No, you can never tell with folk. He got that right.

"Thought I'd send out for a Chinese, if that's ok with you, Tom." Mandy said as she drove through the evening traffic.

"I don't mind, whatever is easiest for you." He said, noticing Mandy was wearing a smart business suit rather than her sexy clothes. She also had less makeup on her face, and he thought she looked more attractive somehow.

When they arrived back at the flat, Mandy parked her car in the underground car park. Each resident had an allocated space but she rarely used hers. She preferred to park it on the short drive in front of her door. But tonight it had to be free for Ken. She and Tom took the stairway to the ground floor flat and Mandy told him to put his luggage in the bedroom. Tom had already had a shower back at the B&B, but Mandy said she wanted to change out of her office clothes and freshen up. She offered to make coffee, but he said he would wait. It was a good half hour before she entered the main room, dressed in black slacks and a black blouse, and her hair pinned up. She phoned to order their evening meal.

"Be about half hour," she said smiling. "How about showing me how to use the online banking system while we wait for it to be delivered."

Tom had hooked his computer bag over his overcoat in the hall cupboard and he went to collect it. Mandy then led him through to the kitchen where they sat side-by-side at the kitchen table. Tom entered a pin number to log on to his laptop. Mandy watched his fingers like a cobra watching a meal and relied on her memory, honed to a high standard by memorising the scripts for different plays. Tom had only used four digits for the pin number and she had no trouble storing them in her memory for further use. Tom used the browser to access his banking app but something went wrong, the image on the screen broke into innumerable pieces like glass shattering. Then the screen went blank.

"What's happened?" Mandy said, looking at Tom with concern.

"Don't know, love. Never happened to me before. Maybe it's because I'm using a different wifi system. Leave it with me and I'll see if I can get it back."

She watched as he shut the computer down and then switched it back on. The screen remained stubbornly blank. Tom frowned at it.

Mandy frowned at it.

"Well? she said, suspiciously.

"I haven't a clue. It may be a fault with the laptop or it may be some security issue with the bank." Tom looked at his watch. "I'll ring the bank tomorrow morning and find out if there's been an issue with their online banking system. If not I'll have to take the laptop to a repairer."

"I thought you were a computer expert?" Mandy was showing her frustration with him and, at the same time thinking you'll not be alive tomorrow you stupid man.

"I'm a programmer, that's software, love. If the problem is my laptop then it will need a hardware expert. You see the screen is blank? I need the machine to be up and running before I can check the software."

"Oh, Christ!" Mandy tried to hide her concern, thinking Ken was going to be furious and probably blame her for failing to get the details of Armstrong's passwords.

At that moment the doorbell rang.

"Do you want me to answer it?" Tom said, closing down the lid on his laptop and rising from the chair.

"Might as well. I want to use the loo." She hurried out of the room.

Mandy stared at herself in the bathroom mirror, and felt like thumping her fist through her image. Her intuition was telling her Tom Armstrong was teasing her, but she couldn't figure out why. Unless of course he had become suspicious of her when she had been questioning him on his personal details and bringing up the subject of his bank accounts. He wasn't stupid she realised. And because he'd seemed easy going she had assumed she could manipulate him at will. As she had done when they'd had sex.

Tom answered the door, took the food, paid for it, and gave the delivery boy a generous tip. He walked back to the kitchen with a thoughtful look on his face.

She left the bathroom and found Tom in the kitchen. He had put the food containers on the counter but had not opened them. "Let's have a look, lover." she said, forcing herself to sound cheerful and pretending to have forgotten all about the computer. "You go and organise yourself a drink to go with this lot. There's a couple of cans of beer in the fridge or there's the drinks cabinet to investigate. I'll just have a large tonic water. "

For the next hour they enjoyed their Chinese and chatted. Mandy kept the conversation light by asking Tom what the video game was about.

"Oh, it's one of those where the hero has special powers to defeat evil. I called him KINSMAN and he wears metal armour that can flex with his muscles. Thought of it a couple of years ago and its taken me this long to get it finished for distribution."

She asked what he would be doing now the video project was finished.

"I have a few other projects pending for other companies. But I intend to take a break for a few weeks. There's some friends who have invited me to stay with them. Nothing settled, but available if I want to take up their offer."

After the meal, Tom helped her clear up which she thought was sweet and almost made her change her mind about tomorrow. But money and Ken were more important and Ken had already hinted what would happen to her if she tried to get out of their arrangement. And this evening it was her job to dispense the correct dose of Ketamine.

"Time for a drink, I think. Whisky again?"

"Yes, please."

Mandy organised the drinks, making sure Tom could not see her adding one Ketamine tablet to his whisky. She handed him his drink and stood until he took a sip. "Alright?" she asked.

"Perfect." He placed his glass on a coaster on the low table.

Mandy used her remote control to bring some slow dance music into the room, and then sat on the opposite sofa, facing Tom. She raised her glass and watched over the rim as he picked his glass and copied her by holding up his glass in a silent toast to her before taking a sip. She crossed her legs and said, "How will you manage without your computer, darling?"

"Oh, I have my mobile. I can use it, if I need money or getting in touch with friends or contacts."

"What about your online accounts?"

"I've decided to leave it until I return to London. I won't need to access them until then. Sorry I couldn't show you how it works. He stared into her eyes, almost as if he was daring her to take the matter further.

She shrugged. "Not important, darling," she said, while thinking the exact opposite. And watched as he took another long sip of his whisky. His glass was almost empty.

Tom sighed and leaned back on the sofa still holding onto his glass. Mandy stood up and leaned forward to take his glass "Another drink, Tom?"

Tom gulped the remaining whisky and

handed her the glass. "Why not," he said, with a merry tone.

Mandy went over to the drinks cabinet and took the remaining tablet from her pocket and mixed it with a large measure of whisky. She did not have to encourage Tom to drink. When she handed him the whisky he took a long gulp and almost emptied the glass.

She sat down again and noticed he was tapping his left hand on his knee to the music while holding his glass in his other hand. He had a sloppy grin on his face and his eyes had started to dilate.

She took a chance and asked, "Did you crash your computer deliberately, Tom?"

He blew a raspberry at her. "What do you think, handy Mandy." he said, then laughed that tailed off in a giggle.

"Care to tell me how to fix it and access your bank account." She was hoping the drug had loosened his tongue.

He stared across at her looking confused at her question. "Feeling strange," he mumbled, and closed his eyes.

"Just sit there, darling. It could be the Chinese has disagreed with you. I'll get something to settle your stomach." She stood up, cursing him under her breath. She left the room and went to the bedroom where she rang Ken on her mobile.

He answered straight away. "Yes, Mandy."

"He's going under. Where are you?"

"Outside. Just open the door."

Mandy looked in at Tom before going to the door. His head had lolled onto the sofa arm and his body was slack as if he was asleep.

She hurried to let Ken in. He was dressed in dark clothes like her.

He stood over Tom, assessing his condition. Mandy could see by Ken's face he wasn't happy. She rushed to explain what had happened.

"I wasn't able to get the passwords for his computer and bank, darling. And I think he cottoned on to me wanting to get them. His computer crashed and I think he did it deliberately."

"Forget his bloody computer. It's not important at the moment." He leaned down towards Tom. "Tom, wakeup,' he said, and then slapped Tom's face.

Tom's eyelids flickered as if he was trying focus. Ken slapped his face again.

"Come on man, wake yourself."

Tom mumbled something unintelligible and his eyes closed.

"Christ. He's out of it, Mandy. He should be able to stand. You definitely only gave him two tablets?"

"Yes, but he also had the whisky and he drank it fast."

"Bloody wimp," he said, and ran his hand over Tom's pockets until he found the wallet. He opened it to give it a cursory search. He found eighty pounds in cash and a debit card. And also a business card with the London address and an email address. He showed Mandy the debit card. "I'll use this for contactless purchases," he said. Then searched the remaining pocket where he found a key wallet holding three keys. "Key's to his flat, I hope." He slipped the wallet into his own pocket.

"Right then. Give me a hand to get him up."

Between them they hauled Tom upright, but he was like a drunk and sagged between them. Ken, still holding on to Tom, bent down and shifted him into a fireman's lift. "Don't just stand there, get the door!" he said, walking across the room with Tom on his shoulders.

Mandy hurried in front, and opened the doors before Ken reached them. Then they were outside. "Car's unlocked," he gasped. "Just open the back door."

Mandy did as she was told and Ken tipped Tom onto the back seat, shifted him so he was stretched out and then closed the car door. He turned to Mandy and said abruptly, "No time to lose. We need his luggage and computer. Mandy went back inside and came out with Tom's things.

Ken threw the case and computer onto the front passenger seat. "Right", he said. "Get your car and follow me."

Mandy hurried inside the house to get her top coat and car keys. Meanwhile Ken had pulled his car off her drive and sat, waiting for her car to appear out of the underground car park. He kept tapping his fingers impatiently on the steering wheel. Bloody women, he grumbled, take twice as long as men.

As soon as she had her car on the street he took off at a reasonable pace. Traffic was quiet and Mandy was able to follow him easily across town and onto the A57, heading towards the Snake Pass.

It took thirty minutes to reach the Snake and he continued to the top of the Pass to turn the car around, using a lay-by. Then he waited for Mandy to do the same.. He set off back down the pass until they were about thirty yards away from the warning barriers where he parked the car. Mandy pulled her SUV in behind.

The countryside was dark and a mist was

forming, softening the landscape. Ken hoped the mist wouldn't thicken until the job was done because it would make it difficult to see any approaching headlights.

He sprung the bonnet catch as he exited the car and saw Mandy get out of her car. "Hang on a minute ." he said. "I have to loosen the petrol pipe. He'd already practiced slackening the nut. He used a small pocket torch to see what he was doing and used a spanner he took from his coat pocket to do the job. It only took him a few seconds The smell of petrol as it leaked from the pipe, satisfied him the pipe was loose enough. He slammed the bonnet shut and then looked up and down the pass to make sure no traffic was approaching. Tom Armstrong was sprawled on the back seat and hadn't moved during the journey. Ken pulled him half out and with Mandy's help managed to get him from that position into the front driving seat. They were panting and sweating by the time they had him slumped over the steering wheel.

Tom's limbs started to twitch and his head started to nod. "Christ, he's coming out of it," Ken said, and he gave up trying to fix the safety belt around Tom. He made sure the car was in neutral, started the car, released the hand brake and stepped back, closing the door as he did so.

Nothing happened. He pushed Mandy towards her car and told her to get in the passenger seat. He took the driver's seat, switched on the engine and manoeuvred the SUV until he could give the Mercedes a gentle shove. The car started to move. He used Mandy's car to keep pushing and as the Mercedes gained speed he dropped back to watch it crash through the barrier. He carried on driving to the lay-by the other side of the landslip. He had just parked when the Mercedes exploded and shot a fireball into the sky. He got out of the car and walked back to see the car burning fiercely. He watched for a few seconds, smiled and returned to Mandy's car.

"Well?" Mandy said.

"It's done, lover chops." And drove off.

CHAPTER 17

Ken couldn't stop chuckling and slapping her thigh as he drove back to her flat. "We've done it, lover-bug. What about that? There won't be anything recognisable left of bloody Tom Armstrong. I hope he was blown to bits."

Mandy was despondent. It was one thing to think of murder, it was soul destroying to actually commit murder. She was feeling sick inside and she had a headache developing behind her eyes making her squint. She was seeing in Ken an unnatural and ugly trait. He actually took great enjoyment in murdering someone. Who is this man, she wondered, how could he have fooled me for so long? And she shivered, realising he would murder her if she threatened him in any way. He was a psychopath! She looked across at him, and in the dim lights from the street lamps they passed, saw the almost perpetual grin on his face. She could see from his attitude she would be a virtual prisoner from now on. What was the use of all that money if my life is under constant threat? How long will I survive? How long before I start to go mad?

"You are quiet, Mandy Sitwell. What's up?"

"Just tired, darling. What with humping Armstrong around. Not what I'm used to."

"What about me?" he said, abruptly. "I've still got the drive to Filey. You'll be tucked up in that fancy bed of yours."

"That's true. Would you like to stay over and do the journey in the morning?"

"No, too risky now I've killed myself and become Tom Armstrong. I might bump into someone who knows me as Ken Birkenshaw. "I'll lie low at that holiday home until Monday then I'll head down to his flat and use his passport so I can move abroad."

Mandy noted the 'I' and with her morbid thoughts cautioning her against correcting him she just said, "I understand."

A short while later they arrived at the car park where his new Range Rover had been kept. His luggage was already stowed away. Ken leaned towards her and gave a hard bruising kiss on her lips.

"Let me know any news on the accident as soon as possible, lover-bug." he said as he slipped from her car. Mandy opened the passenger door, walked around to the driving side and watched Ken drive away before putting her car in gear and driving out of the car park.

She went back to the flat and washed the glasses she and Tom had used. Then she made herself a weak whisky and sat down on the sofa she had used when Tom was with her. A melancholy emotion overwhelmed her. Tom Armstrong had made more of an impression on her than she had realised. There had been a freshness, an inno-cent abroad attitude she now found was a marked contrast to Ken's blatant villainy. Oh, God, she thought, i think the wrong man died tonight.

She felt even worse when she looked across at the sofa he had used. It was as if he was still pre-sent in her flat. She quickly walked to her bed-room, sank down onto the bed and cried quietly for several minutes. It was not for Tom, but for herself. What a stupid fool she had been to think money was more important than a man's life. When she had calmed down she had a long shower, trying to scrub her mind as clean as her body. She finally lay in bed and let the events of the even-ing run through her mind,, wondering if she would ever be free of Ken; and the guilt of Tom's murder. Eventually she fell into a troubled sleep, waking several times from the nightmare of seeing Tom fleeing from a burning car engulfed in flames.

Mandy was a serial reader of social media and on Saturday morning she found Twitter had de-tails from an eye witness of a car accident on the Snake Pass. A car had exploded in flames and a man, assumed to be the driver, had been thrown from the car and was seriously injured. He had been taken to the Western General hospital and was in intensive care. The police were trying to identify the injured man. When she read it she started to laugh hysterically, then had a choking fit and gasped for breath. God, all that guilt, all those nightmares and he was still alive. She knew Tom Armstrong was going to live no matter how serious his injuries. There was an Archangel looking after him. And she also knew when Ken Birkenshaw heard her news he would be absolutely furious. All their plans had gone up in smoke. An ironic joke, and she couldn't help the smile spreading across her face. Another Archangel had decided to give her life back. She was determined to make the most of it. Bugger the money. Getting away from Ken Birkenshaw would be a matter of deceit and feminine guile. And she was prepared to use any method if it saved her from murder; the murder of Tom or the murder of herself.

She phoned Ken's mobile number. When his sleepy voice answered she told him the news. She then had to hold the phone away from her ear as the expletives came pouring out. It took Birkenshaw well over a minute before he'd calmed down enough to say he would be back over to her place by lunchtime.

Mandy could only acquiesce.

"And I need you to use your artistic skills on me, Mandy. Your very best skills. Do you hear?"

"I hear, darling." She would have to be patient

and bide her time.

Ken arrived at her flat just after noon. "Show me," he said.

Mandy handed over her tablet that showed him the social media article on the car accident. When he'd finished reading he handed the tablet back. She brought up another article that had appeared later in the morning. This one was from an unknown source at Western General, stating the patient was in intensive care but was stable. Ken read it and his face hardened. "I'll give him bloody stable. What I want to know is how that bloody nerd survived the explosion, and how he was thrown from the blazing car."

Mandy tried to look as sympathetic as possible when she shrugged her shoulders. "Luck of the devil, perhaps." As soon as she said it, she knew she'd said the wrong thing."

"Luck of the devil, you bloody think!" He stormed, catching her by the shoulder and shaking her until her teeth rattled. "The devil would have let him die, you stupid fool. And all I want from you is how we are going to kill him before he recovers." He almost threw her from him, causing her to stumble onto one of the sofas.

Mandy looked up at him, shocked from both the shaking and the absurdity of his thinking. "You can't possibly think you can kill him while he is in the intensive care unit, Ken?"

"Why not? If he blabs when he wakes up, I'll be on the run for the rest of my life."

"Better that, than going to prison for murder, don't you think."

He strode up and down the room, thumping a fist into the palm of his other hand. Mandy watched as he finally gained control of his anger. He stopped and sat abruptly on the other sofa, his blue eyes hooded and hard.

"You are probably right," he eventually grunted, "But it's a thought."

"Why not wait and see what happens. He's seriously injured and he may not recover. Or if he does, the injuries and the Ketamine may have affected his brain."

"Be too late to do anything then because people will know he's not me."

"Well, we can go back to our original plan, darling. I'll create a disguise for you and you'll have to pay someone to give you another identity." she said, trying to coax him away from his murderous thoughts.

"We'll need to have some inside information," he muttered to himself. "We can use the mobile I gave Clair. That will tell us if she thinks Armstrong is me and how he's recovering. Yes, inside information, it will give us an edge. But we'll need more listening devices for the house just to make certain we have every thing covered."

Mandy was relieved he was thinking more reasonably. "I agree darling. Shall we organise the disguise, now?"

CHAPTER 18

Ken, in his disguise, looked entirely different from his normal appearance. Mandy had dyed his hair a light brown. He wore a matching false beard, and a pair of tinted spectacles that altered the colour of his eyes and, lastly, some inserts to wear in his mouth to fill out his cheeks, but he decided the inserts were too uncomfortable to wear. He instructed Mandy to contact the security firm they did business with and to buy three top of the range listening devices, one for each of the main down stairs rooms in the house. They had already decided, when they were planning the theft, it was best for her to remain as secretary to Richard after Ken had stolen the money. She would then hand in her notice about a month after the event and follow him abroad. This would reduce the suspicion that she was in involved in the operation. It would also be an opportunity for them to know what Richard intended to do to try to recover the money. Mandy was not looking forward to turning up for work on Monday morning. Especially with Ken ordering her to keep her eyes and ears wide open for any relevant information. Fine for you, she thought. You could scarper any time now you have the money and leave me high and dry. She had a shock in the afternoon when there was a knock on her office door and Mrs White, the office

Supervisor, stuck her head in. "Sorry to bother you, Mandy, but there's a Police Officer wanting to see someone in charge."

Mandy sat, trying to keep her face expressionless and free of guilt. "What about?"

"A car accident involving Mr Birkenshaw."

Mandy, thought for a moment, well at least she would have more information about Tom. "Alright, show him in."

Mrs White showed the Constable in. He was young, fresh faced and carried his hat under his arm. "Constable Turner, Miss Sitwell. I've been sent to inquire about Mr Birkenshaw. You do know he was involved in a serious car accident?"

Mandy frowned. "No, I don't know anything about a car accident involving Ken....Mr Birkenshaw."

Mandy saw the Constable grit his teeth before he closed his mouth over them, thinning his lips. It looked as if he'd wanted to swear and was making an effort to control himself. He took a deep breath. "I'm sorry. I assumed you knew. Mr Birkenshaw was involved in a car accident on the Snake Pass on Friday evening. He was thrown from the car and the car caught fire. He is now in the Western General intensive care unit."

Mandy tried to look shocked. She looked at

Turner. "What sort of injuries?"

"He has suffered a head trauma. And he's unconscious. There's not a lot more I can tell you."

"You say he was thrown from the car and it caught fire."

"Yes, that's what we are assuming from the evidence. Mr Birkenshaw had no burn marks, which he would have had if he'd been near the car when it caught fire."

Mandy was trying to think of obvious questions to ask. "Was there anyone else....his wife, Clair?"

"No. No one else was involved." Constable Turner took a notebook out of a breast pocket in his tunic. "We are trying to gather information on the cause of the accident. Could I ask you a few questions?"

Guilt made Mandy's heart skip a beat. "What sort of information?"

"HIs mental state, if possible? Was he stressed through work? Does he have money worries?"

"Why. Why the personal information?" Mandy was getting angry.

"We are just trying to establish the cause of the accident, Miss. And having more information regarding Mr Birkenshaw will help. And I assure you any information you supply will be kept strictly confidential."

Mandy was determined to avoid any questioning at all costs. She could trip herself up, knowing it was Tom Armstrong and not Ken Birkenshaw lying in that hospital bed. "Sorry Constable but I can't help you. Mr Birkenshaw is one of the Directors and I'm not privy to his thoughts or mental state. You will have to wait until Mr Cartwright returns. He will be back a week today."

Constable Turner stared hard at her. She stared blandly back at him. Finally he put his book away. "Good day, Miss Sitwell."

Ken Birkenshaw used the parking area where hikers were fond of leaving their cars. It was ideal, partly hidden from the road and only a mile from the house. He had bought himself some cheap outdoor clothes, including a pair of hiking boots to wear across the boggy fields and the two hills hiding the old farmhouse from view. There was a small wood overlooking the house and he stayed in the shadows to observe the property. Iris's car was parked behind a police car. He couldn't have timed his visit better. He hoped Clair was carrying her mobile where she usually did or had it in close proximity to her. He dug out is own mobile and dialled up the listening device on the live channel. The reception was clear and not muffled by Clair's pocket so he guessed she had put it down somewhere or she had it on charge in the kitchen. The good thing was he could hear the conversation between Clair, Iris and the police officer as if he was in the room with them. The Police Officer was explaining about the accident. Ken concentrated:

"No, he's not dead, but he was seriously injured and taken to Western General. I thought you knew....." The Police Officer went on to explain the delay in Clair being informed. And that her husband was in a stable condition.

Ken was surprised and pleased at how concerned Clair sounded over his injuries. She should have been pleased he had nearly died after their row on Friday. He continued to listen and was especially interested when they discussed how Tom Armstrong had been thrown clear of the car before the car exploded. Armstrong had been extraordinary lucky to escape with his life! He heard Clair say she was going to ring the hospital but he didn't hear the conversation. He guessed she had left the room to ring on the landline in the garden room. It made him realise the mobile listening device had a drawback. Clair had to be carrying the phone or be close to it. When Ken heard Clair say he was in a coma and she was visiting that afternoon, he rang off and hiked back to his car.

On the journey to Mandy's flat he thought about the problem of Armstrong surviving, but happy he had a bit of time to think of a solution. And also time to install more listening devices in the house instead of relying on the mobile. Hopefully he would hear of an opportunity to kill the bastard.

CHAPTER 19

When Mandy came in from work, she said, "I had a visit from the law this afternoon. A Constable Turner. He more or less...

Ken interrupted her and explained how he'd heard Tom Armstrong was in a coma. And he played the mobile recording from start to finish. "Bit of luck he's in a coma. Don't you think, lover-bee?"

"Yes, darling. Lucky for you too, you could listen to their conversation." Mandy went to her shoulder bag and took out the package of listening devices she had been given by the security firm. "Here, a few more of your gadgets. Hope they will be as useful. They cost the earth."

Ken took the package and looked at the devices. There was a note from his contact. "These are expensive because they will not be found by a scanner when listening. They will be found if they are sending and a professional scanner is used."

Ken handed the note to Mandy. "They could be our salvation, Mandy. The mobile can be found using a scanning app."

"Salvation? What do you mean, darling?"

"I really need his identity. It will make my life

easier. It's as simple as that."

Mandy realised Ken had become obsessed with Tom's identity. And she knew he would kill Tom if an opportunity arose. Oh God, she was in a relationship with a monster. A thought fluttered on the border of her mind that informing the police would be the best way to stop him. But what proof did she have? And now knowing what Ken was capable of, he would make sure she was brought down with him.

The next day Ken headed for the old farm, armed with the listening devices.

He had timed his arrival at his observation spot just before he thought Clair was due to visit the hospital. He was relying on Clair's obsession with being on time for her to leave the house around one thirty for the 2pm visiting session.

He saw Clair had her car out of the garage and parked by the front door. He sat against one of the beech trees to wait and when he was comfortable he cast his eyes over the land surrounding the farm. He was blind to the scenery. Certainly not interested in the splendour of the majestic beech, the massive chestnut or the silver birch, all just starting to show a haze of green with their opening buds. He was calculating how many houses could be built. Not the modern cheapies crowded together, but luxury stockbroker houses, each with sufficient land to save some trees and satisfy the blasted eco warriors. Eco wimps more like. He was sidetrack for a moment thinking of all those protesters he'd had to fight with guile and deceit. Didn't they realise it was men like him who provided the houses they forgot they needed when marching with their silly placards. He turned his head to take in the moorland views sweeping upward into the foothills of the Pennines, the Backbone of England, where thousands, from all over, were drawn to every year to hike the Pennie Way. Silly buggers!

God, he could have made seven or eight million, easily. It would have been the ideal development plan that would have solved his money problems, put him back on his feet and not had him turning his mind to theft. But bloody Clair had refused even to think about it. When they first met and he saw how much she adored him, he thought it would be easy, with his well practiced charm offensive to convince her of his property plans. He hadn't realised beneath her romantic nature there was a core of steel.

The sky was overcast with grey cloud threatening rain and he was pleased with his outdoor gear that kept out the cold wind skittering through the trees. Ten minutes later Clair emerged and drove off. He set off down the hill, feeling in his coat pocket for the house keys. He used the back door to enter the house and moved quickly to the security panel to turn off the alarm.

At least he could rely on Clair to leave the security codes alone.

He'd already decided to use the landline phone in the garden room to place one of the devices. The phone was a retro of one of the early phones and Ken quickly unscrewed the base with one of the screwdrivers he'd brought with him. He inserted the `device and screwed the base back on. He returned to the kitchen and used one of the kitchen chairs to give him the height to place a device on top of one of the wall units. Each of the devices had a magnetic strip and a sticky tape strip, but he didn't need to use either. Then on to the dining room for the third device where he used the magnetic strip to clamp it to one of the metal brackets holding a table leg.

Satisfied, he tested each device by dialling up their numbers from a list that came with the devices. He used the same phrase for each test. "Hi, Clair, this is your loving husband. Hope you miss me." He was halfway out of the house when he remembered he hadn't turned on the security alarm. He chided himself to concentrate on what he was doing instead of congratulating himself on a simple job. He went back to the panel and turned the alarm on.

Despite the cold weather he was sweating when he got back to the Range Rover. He sat for a moment before starting the car and thought of

Tom Armstrong. From what he'd heard already the lucky bastard was going to survive. Was it worth hanging about to see if an opportunity arose to kill him? The punishment for murder was far higher than for stealing the money. He could chose virtually any country to make a run for it. And with a good disguise and a perfect false identity he'd be laughing all the way to the bank. But was there a perfect disguise? And where could he get a decent new identity? It was obvious, changing places with Tom Armstrong! It was the threat of Richard Cartwright hiring expert investigators, not law enforcement that worried him. He knew the man, knew he would never stop hunting to recover the millions on principle. He would hate the thought of Ken Birkenshaw getting away with making a fool of him. He sighed, he'd wait a while longer. With the listening devices in place he would know Armstrong's progress.

For the first three days of him listening to Clair's conversations, Armstrong remained in a coma. On the third day he heard Clair tell Iris Armstrong seemed to be regaining consciousness. And when she told her sister Armstrong seemed to recognise her, Ken swore and reported the development to Mandy.

She advised he should start to flee. He shook his head. "Before I do that, I'll need a new identity to leave the country."

He could have kicked himself for not doing something about it sooner, but he been so certain he could become Tom Armstrong he'd given it only an occasional thought. In fact, on those occasions he had thought about a new identity he didn't know how to go about it. He'd heard stories of villains taking on a new identity, but the nitty gritty of how had escaped him so far.

He didn't sleep too well that night but come the next afternoon when he heard Dr Miller telling Clair Armstrong had psychogenic amnesia he thought his luck was finally changing. From then on, either he or Mandy used the mobile to listen to the recordings from the various devices Ken had planted in the house or to Clair's mobile. That mobile had proved a godsend, despite the fact the reception was muted when Clair's clothes dampened down the clarity of conversations. Ken couldn't contain his good humour and Mandy would have been pleased he'd become easier to live with, except she knew he was gnawing away at the possibility of killing Tom.

His good humour did slip a few notches when he heard Iris rubbish his character and Mandy heard him mutter to himself, given a chance he would get her too. She shivered. Ken was becoming unhinged since the fiasco of the Snake Pass. Depression lurked almost constantly in her mind she had stress from having to go to work, knowing the theft of the money would be discovered when Richard returned from holiday causing her to take sleeping tablets to get a night's sleep.

On the following Monday Mandy came home from work to find Ken flopped on the sofa and a far away look in his eyes. "What's up, sweetheart?"

"Clair's collecting him from the hospital tomorrow. And he still hasn't recovered his memory. And do you know what. Clair still hasn't realised he isn't me. How lucky can I get, lover-bug?"

"I find that extraordinary, sweetheart. I'd certainly see the difference between you and him."

"Ah but you know there are two of us. She doesn't. And she's been told, by an expert, mark you, Armstrong could've created a whole new personality. It's hilarious, isn't it, darling?"

"That's the first time you've called me, darling, Ken."

"Slip of the tongue, lover-bee."

"Richard came back from his holiday today. Had you forgotten?"

"No I hadn't. Has he had a heart attack?'

"No. But he quizzed me for a hour. Talk about 1984. I thought I was in room 101. Wanted to know if I was aware of the missing money. If you and me were in a relationship. I have a feeling, Ken, he didn't quite believe me."

"Don't matter what he thinks, sweet pea," Ken said, giving her a sly look. "I only wish I was a fly on the wall. I'd have loved to see his face."

"Well, I think he'll want to talk to Tom Armstrong as soon as he can."

"Agreed. So we'd better keep on listening, flower."

"Can I hand in my notice? It's doing my head in going into that place every day. Bad enough when Richard was away. But now he's back it's ten times worse."

"No you can't, Mandy. Just keep your bloody nerve you are going to be rich enough."

Mandy, opened her mouth, but then snapped it shut and went to have a long hot shower.

CHAPTER 20

It became his habit to stay in the flat most of the day while Mandy was at work and play the recordings from the listening devices nearly every hour. In the evenings he usually played any recordings he hadn't heard by staying up after Mandy had retired. The only good thing about Armstrong staying with Clair at the farmhouse was his memory failing to return. Listening to the recordings of Armstrong and Clair becoming lovers incensed him, His jealously sparked a murderous rage that if Armstrong and Clair had been within reach he would have strangled both of them with his bare hands, He was glad Mandy had retired to bed when he listened to Armstrong and Clair making love in the garden room. He knew he would have expended his rage on her. He stayed up and drank his way through nearly a full bottle of whisky and fell asleep on the sofa. And that's where Mandy found him the following morning, mouth open and snoring like a formula one Red Bull car. An empty whisky bottle on the floor beside the sofa told her to leave him to recover on his own.

He awoke with a terrible headache that took all morning and four paracetamol to become bearable. It didn't help when he heard Clair agree to Richard Cartwright visiting and interviewing

Armstrong at two o'clock. And when he heard Cartwright's ultimatum for Armstrong to return the money or else, then he had to leave the flat before his rage destroyed it. He drove to his usual parking spot after leaving the flat and the drive helped to calm him down. He started analysing the problem of how to stop this runaway disaster destroying his plans. It was no longer a matter of the nerd regaining his memory, it was making sure everyone thought Armstrong was Ken Birkenshaw when Cartwright called in the police.

He took out his mobile and activated the call back facility for the mobile phone he had given Clair. The mobile had recorded Clair saying she was walking to Millward to buy some milk. Armstrong asked if he could come. Ken switched off the mobile, thought for a minute, debating with himself whether the risk was worth it. This was not the ideal opportunity. Once the job was done he'd have to cart the Armstrong's body away and think of some way to dispose of it. Bloody fingerprints. But at least he had an opportunity to save his plan of stealing Armstrong's identity. I know the route she'll take. Always the same. If I go now I'll be there before them. Go for it, man.

It took him ten minutes to get in position. Exactly seven minutes later they walked past the Range Rover. He waited until they were about halfway along the straight. He started the Range Rover, pulled out of the passing place, and accelerated towards them. He saw Armstrong look over his shoulder, grab Clair and lift her to safety. "Don't care a ducks arse about her, you snivelling git," he muttered, and pressed the accelerator to the floor. He thought Armstrong would make a run for it and his hunter's instinct brought a smile to his lips Then Armstrong gave a two fingered gesture. "Right you bastard!" he shouted, his voice extraordinary loud inside the cab and braced himself for the impact of steel against flesh.

Armstrong disappeared from view...no impact..."What the hell?" He looked in the rearview mirror. Armstrong was sitting up in the middle of the road, Clair sliding down the embankment.

"How the bloody hell did he do it?" He hammered his fist on the Range Rover's steering wheel with frustrated rage. "He should be bloody dead!" He was so inflamed he didn't realise the bend was coming up so fast and braked hard to avoid a serious accident. The Range Rover tilted on two wheels as he spun the steering wheel and his heart skipped a beat. The near accident calmed his rage but not his frustration.

He was in two minds whether to go back or not. In the end he thought it best to get away from the area in case they called the police.

On the journey back to Mandy's flat his rage kept bubbling up and it was only with a major effort of will power he kept a lid on it. He couldn't help himself, his thoughts kept coming back to Tom bloody Armstrong. That man must have the luck of the devil. The car accident on the Snake Pass had been carefully planned, and with Mandy's help they had manipulated Armstrong to certain death by fire. He had watched the car burst into flames, He had watched the explosion but he had not seen how that bastard had escaped from the car.

The same today, even though the murder had been a spur of the moment decision it should have been fail safe. But Armstrong had outwitted him with sheer bravado. Who would have thought a computer nerd had the guts to stand in front of a Range Rover and wait until the last moment to throw himself out of the way to escape death. Unbelievable! He would have to come up with another plan to see Armstrong dead and no longer a threat. He thought it best not to say anything to Mandy. He knew from her remarks she didn't want to get involved in any further murder attempts. Maybe he should think about finalising her as well.

Back at the flat the first thing he did was activate the mobile listening device. It failed to answer. He tried the in the kitchen. Clair was just telling Armstrong she'd ring Iris and ask if they could stay with her. Ken rang the device hidden in the landline phone, knowing Clair preferred to use that one when at home. He heard the phone ring Iris's number and then listened to Clair explain what had happened to her and Tom.

Ken nearly threw his mobile across the room when he heard her use Armstrong's name and then his stomach lurched when Clair told her sister she suspected her husband of trying kill them and they would go to the police the following morning. When Clair finished her call and went back to the kitchen, he rang the device again and listened to the conversation between Armstrong and her. When they were finished he put his mobile away and stood in the middle of the room. Christ, his murder attempt had blown up in his face. He would have to make a run for it. And then an icy calm froze his emotions. Ok, if he had to make a run for it, fine. But he'd make sure Armstrong would be dead before he left. He decided he needed a shower and his thinking cap.

CHAPTER 21

Ken allowed the hot water to flow over him as he let his thoughts flow over the problem of a new identity, good enough to allow him to flee the country. It would be a must because once the police knew he'd stolen the money and tried to murder Armstrong, his chances of escaping abroad were almost zero. He started to dry off when he remembered the gun. Oh, bloody heck, he thought, what a stupid fool he'd been, trying to make the attempted murders look like an accident. He should have done it differently. Made it look like a gangster killing. A falling out of villains over the money. The gun was the answer to stealing Tom Armstrong's identity.

He finished towelling dry and changed into his dark clothes. Thinking through the details of his latest murder plan he was unemotional and let his brain take over. He only felt this cool and calculating when planning a murder. Like when he was twelve and had murdered his mother and stepfather by increasing the purity of their drugs. He had often contemplated the murder of business rivals from time to time but that had merely led to making sure they lost more money than they gained. But trying to kill the nerdy Armstrong was proving to be bloody difficult. But this time there would be no fancy planning. It would be direct and to the point. Just thinking about it, kindled his emotions again, but not anger, no, this time it was the raw excitement and pleasure of murdering someone.

Mandy had been staying later at the office and he knew she wanted to avoid his ever changing moods. He rang her and she left it ring for nearly a minute before answering.

"Mandy, I want to check something in Richard's office, Wait for me."

"Tell me what what you want, darling. I'll do it for you. Save you the trip."

"Thanks for the offer. But I need to check it myself. Just stay there and wait for me." He kept his tone firm, and Mandy knew not to argue.

Mandy had locked the office door for security reasons but she let him in as soon as he rang the bell. Ken swept past her and made for Richard's office. She automatically tried to follow him in.

"No, Mandy," he said. "I'll only be a few minutes." and shut the door on her.

He went over to Richard's safe. He had seen Richard open the safe so many times he'd automatically memorised the code in case he ever needed it. He opened the safe, reached inside and took out the revolver that was a war memento from Richard's grandfather. He had hung on to it when he left the army after serving as an officer during WWII. The revolver was in a holster and with it a pouch holding six bullets. Ken took them over to the desk. and examined the revolver. Richard had not particularly looked after it but it was in good order. Ken had been shown it a couple of years back when Richard had taken it out of the safe to get at some documents, and explained it had become a somewhat family heirloom. He kept it in his office safe because of his young children at home.

He took the six bullets from the pouch and loaded the gun, put the holster and pouch back in the safe and the gun into a pocket of his overcoat. It weighed the coat down but at least it was concealed. He left the office and found Mandy back at her desk, but with her jacket on and ready to go home. She stood up when he entered.

"Can I go now?" she said, sarcastically.

"You're coming with me. But we'll use your car."

Mandy opened her mouth to protest but Ken raised his hand to stop her. "I want no argument. Just do as I say, Mandy."

"Why, Ken?"

Ken took the gun out of his pocket, moved in close to her and tapped her on the shoulder with barrel of the revolver. She saw his face harden and his eyes pierced her own. "I said no argument. Now give me your car keys and just get going." His voice had taken on a cold, unemotional tone. It frightened Mandy into obeying without further protest.

He had parked his car in the nearby carpark where Mandy had a permanent slot. It was almost empty and Ken had parked his car next to hers. He pressed Mandy's remote control to open the doors and without a word waited for her to get in before walking to his car, opening the boot and taking out a laptop in a bag and a briefcase. He walked back to Mandy's car and put computer and brief-case into the car boot He stood for a moment scanning the carpark and the street beyond before climbing into the driving seat.

"Where are we going?" Mandy asked as Ken drove out of the carpark and headed out of the city.

"A little visit to Iris King. Now shut up because I want to think."

He went over his plan again. Get all the people who knew Tom Armstrong had been set up to take his place together in one room. Shoot them all and set the house on fire. He now had the means and the will to carry out the triple murder. No, four murders, he almost forgot Mandy It was simple and he assured himself, foolproof. He would miss Clair and Mandy, but the satisfaction gained from doing away with the other two would make up for it.

Mandy was becoming more frightened of him by the minute. He had become a stranger to her. His face looked etched in stone, his emotionless tone of voice and those piercing blue eyes when he'd stared at her before leaving the office made her think he'd finally lost all reason. She had the awful feeling the nightmare was just beginning.

He stopped the car a little way from the gateway into Iris's drive but didn't turn off the engine. "Now, Mandy. When we get to the front door, you stand where the security camera can see you and press the bell and smile that cheesy smile of yours when Iris answers. That's all I want you to do. Got it?"

Mandy found she had lost the ability to speak and nodded instead.

Ken put the car in gear and drove through the gateway, up to the front door and parked next to Clair's Honda. They both got out of the car. Mandy walked up to the front door, and nearly jumped out of her skin when an automatic motion system switched the security light on. She glanced up and saw a security camera focused on her, and pressed the bell.

Ken stood slightly behind her, and bent at his

knees slightly to make himself look smaller. He gripped the gun in his pocket. They had to wait a couple of minutes before the door opened and Mandy was surprised to see Tom Armstrong's unsmiling face staring at her.

"Tom?"

Ken shoved her in the back so hard she stumbled towards Tom and he took a step back but put up his hands to stop her falling. She received another push from Ken to keep her going and then he followed her in and shut the door behind him.

Tom Armstrong smiled, thinking it was some sort of joke. But when the gun lifted until he was staring down the muzzle, his smiled drained away.

"What's so funny, Armstrong?" Ken said,

Tom just shook his head. "Sorry, thought it was joke. Are you Ken Birkenshaw? You don't look like me."

Ken didn't answer the question, but snarled, "You'll not think it's a joke when this gun puts a bloody bullet in you." Now move back where my lovely wife and her shitty sister are."

"If it's me you want then I'll come with you. No need to bother the girls." Tom said in a reasonable tone.

"Don't you start giving me orders you nerdy prick. Now move!"

Tom held his ground.

Mandy glanced at Ken. It was enough for her to turn back to Tom and say, "Do as he says, Tom. Or he'll shoot you on the spot."

Tom, without another word, turned and headed back to Iris's dining room.

Mandy and Ken followed. Ken, holding the gun down by his side until they entered the room, then he brought it up to cover his wife and his sister-in-law. Iris was standing by the marble fireplace and Clair was sitting at the far end of the dining table staring at him with a puzzled look on her face.

Ken whipped off the spectacles, "Hello, Clair, sweetheart. Miss me?"

She recognised the blue eyes and saw it was her husband behind the beard and brown hair. But his voice sounded unfamiliar, there was a hard cutting edge to it.

Ken saw her confusion and smiled. Clair saw the smile didn't warm the ice in his eyes. And now he had a gun in his hand she knew she would be lucky to leave this room alive.

"What do you want, Ken?" Iris said, Her tone of voice matching his."

"Entertainment." Ken said, a sardonic grin twisting his lips.

"Go to bloody hell," Iris shouted and threw the iron poker she'd been hiding behind her back at him with all her strength.

Ken stepped to one side to let the poker sail harmlessly by and take a chunk of plaster out of the wall behind him. He raised the gun to shoot Iris.

Tom didn't see this, Mandy was now between him and Birkenshaw, he had a massive adrenaline rush, the same as when he was threatened by the Range Rover. The urge for action took over his body and he launched himself at Mandy, carrying her with the force of a rugby tackle into Ken and knocking him flying against the wall. The sound of the gun going off was deafening. The bullet thunked into the ceiling, sending a piece of plaster flying across the room Tom pulled Mandy out of the way and struck at Ken's wrist as the gun was coming to bear on him. The blow knocked the arm sideways and the front sight of the gun caught in the opening of Ken's overcoat. He wrenched the gun to pull it free. At the same time his finger pressed the trigger. The cylinder turned, the firing pin struck the live round and blasted the bullet into his stomach.

The agonising pain as the bullet tore through his vital organs crumpled Ken to his knees. The gun dropped from his hand. He gripped Tom's arm and looked up. Tom bent over and held him.

Ken saw himself in Tom's features and as his eyes dimmed, he said with his last breath, "I...should...be...you...."

Tom eased Ken to the floor next to the gun. He almost picked it up, intending to put it safely out of the way. But then decided it would be best not to disturb the crime scene. He stood up and glanced at Clair. She looked frozen, her eyes round with the horror at seeing her husband die in front of her. Tom walked over and said, "I really didn't mean for this to happen, sweetheart."

She took her eyes off her husband and touched Tom's face lightly. "It wasn't your fault, Tom. I saw he was trying to shoot you."

"He tried to shoot me too, Tom." Iris, said, adding to Clair's assurance. She then picked her up her phone and dialled emergency services. When the call was answered she explained a man had shot himself and gave the necessary details.

Mandy stepped forward and looked down at Ken, and said, "He was going to kill us all. He forced me to come with him." Tom noticed Mandy walked with a limp.

"Why on earth would he want to do that!" Clair said, shocked her husband could contemplate such a thing.

"We were the only ones who knew he was identical to Tom and was going to use the fact to change places with him."

"Yes," Tom said, "And you assisted him, Mandy. You drugged me, didn't you?"

"Only because he threatened to kill me if I didn't do as he asked. And I was really glad you survived the accident. Honestly."

"That's difficult to believe. Anyway, what's the matter with your leg. You're limping."

Mandy touched her knee. "I hurt it when you tackled me into Ken." She shrugged. "Could have been worse. He could have shot me."

"I think I can hear sirens." Clair said.

They all listened. Iris said, "I'll go and let them in."

"I don't want to stay in this room. I'll be in the sitting room," Clair said. And the rest of them followed her. Iris shut the door behind her and then walked to her front door to let the paramedics and the police in. She led them back to her dining room and explained briefly what had happened. She then left them to it and joined the others in the sitting room.

For the next few hours the house filled with official figures from various departments; Paramedics, Scene of Crime Officers (SOCO) and police investigators.

While they were being interviewed separately, Ken's body was taken away and the SOCO team finished their examination of the dining room, sealing it with scene of the crime tape when they left.

The lead detective, Inspector Jones had a neat moustache, intelligent grey eyes and was quietly spoken. He issued a warning that he would need to interview them further over the next few days and not to leave the area without first notifying him.

They were all shattered when the last vehicle drove away. Iris said to Tom and Clair the offer to stay was still available and then she turned to Mandy who was sitting on a settee next to Tom. "I can see you are in no fit state to drive, either How's that knee? "

Mandy bent her knee and winced. "Getting better, I think. But still a bit sore."

"Best you stay too, then."

Mandy accepted and tried to give Tom a kiss on the cheek before she stood to follow Iris out of the room and looked hurt when he moved away from her.

Clair, sitting on the other settee, saw the action and knew why he'd done it. She waited until Iris and Mandy had left the room and explained to Tom she was going to sleep with Iris.

Tom gazed at her in bemusement and saw her lip trembling. He guessed she was still in shock at what happened to Ken and he could see now she was an emotional wreck. He put his arms around her. "It's ok sweetheart, I understand."

CHAPTER 22

Tom was disappointed Clair had decided to sleep with her sister and not with him. On the other hand, he could understand she had gone through a traumatic experienced of watching her husband die in front of her. He lay in bed in one of the spare rooms and wondered if looking exactly like Ken Birkenshaw could be the main reason Clair didn't want to sleep with him.

The following morning, Iris, Clair and Tom were having breakfast together. Mandy had asked Iris if she could lie in. The three of them discussed the events of the previous night.

"I really couldn't recognise Ken as the man I'd married. And I'm not talking about his disguise, it was his cruel attitude. The way he nearly shot you Iris and then Tom. He was like a mad man."

"I always told you, love, he was the most deceitful man I'd ever met. And now I think he was a psychopath. You were lucky he killed himself last night."

"It was an accident, Iris." Tom said

"Best accident that could have happened." Iris said.

"Oh, that's a terrible thing to say." Clair said.

"There you go again. Trying to defend that monster."

"No, Iris. I know now how bad he was, but he was completely different when I married him. He was charming and romantic and made me feel special."

"Yeh, and he tried to have sex with me on your wedding day."

"Alright, Iris, have it your way." Clair said as she stood up and walked out of the room.

Tom stood up to follow her, but Iris said, "I'd leave her alone for the moment, Tom. Clair was totally blind to Ken Birkenshaw's faults. She was in love with the man and it's difficult for her to come to terms with the fact he was a psychopath."

Tom sat down again. "I know you're right. Clair is the most loyal girl I've met. It's one of the reasons I'm in love with her. Pity I remind her so much of Birkenshaw."

"Don't be silly, Tom. Clair has already fallen in love with you. And although I've only known you since yesterday, you are the complete opposite of that man. I saw how you put your life on the line for all of us last night."

Tom hoped she was right. "Well you throwing that poker helped. And him stepping aside gave me the chance to bring him down."

"No, Tom. Looking back it was a reckless and stupid act and give him a reason to start shooting us."

"I don't think he wanted a reason, Iris. Mandy had it right, he was going to shoot us all. And you were right by saying he was a psychopath."

Iris's landline phone rang just as Clair returned and Mandy walked in behind her, looking as if she'd made an attempt to freshen up but not succeeding entirely due to the state of her business suit. It was creased and marked from the scuffle with Ken Birkenshaw. She still had a bit of a limp.

The phone call was from Inspector Jones, He wanted to make an appointment to interview her, Clair and Tom the following day. He could do the interview at her house or they could come to the station, whichever they preferred. Iris opted for her house, and asked if they would need a solicitor present. Inspector Jones assured her it wouldn't be necessary. All he wanted was a more detailed account of the events leading up to the death of Ken Birkenshaw.

Iris conveyed the message. Mandy glanced at Tom and saw his face harden, killing the smile she was about to give him. But she was desperate to have a word with him.

"Where's my computer, phone and tablet, Mandy? And while we're at it, where's my luggage?"

Mandy went white. She could see Tom was not the same innocent she had manipulated into her bed or the vulnerable bloke she had drugged. If he told Inspector Jones what she had done in helping Ken Birkenshaw she would be facing a long term in prison. She looked around at Clair and Iris and saw they were staring at her, waiting for a reply. She breathed in deeply, as if readying herself for going to the bottom of a very deep and murky pool.

"Ken put them in the car with you, Tom. They were probably destroyed in the fire."

"Why would Ken do that?" Clair asked before Tom could say anything.

"He was upset when he couldn't get into computer and phone because of the passwords. Look Tom, could I have a word with you alone?"

"Why?" His tone was abrupt.

"Please, Tom. It's important."

"Whatever it is you can tell me in here."

Mandy saw he was determined and knew it was pointless to argue but still hesitated not wanting Clair and Iris to hear what she was going to discuss with Tom. She took another deep breath, this one for an even murkier pool.

"Tom, I know I've done wrong to you and I'm

truly sorry. And I'm really glad you survived the attempted murder."

"But you were party to it, Mandy. I can't see the difference."

"I know, Tom. I didn't mean it that way. It also made me realise what an evil thing I'd done in assisting Ken Birkenshaw and how lucky I am you weren't killed."

"Alright, Mandy. What do you want?"

"Forgiveness would help. I still feel guilty about helping Ken. And if you can keep quiet about me helping him then I'll help you to get the money back."

"How can you do that?"

"I know the account number and passwords where Ken put the Money. And if you can pretend you found the details yourself so Richard Cartwright need not know I was involved."

"You are trying to manipulate me again, Mandy. Like you did when Ken was alive."

"Not manipulating, Tom. I'm just trying to save myself from going to prison."

"Where is Ken's computer, the one he used to transfer the money?"

"It's in the boot. I'll get it for you." Mandy stood and went to fetch the computer from the car.

"What do you think?" Tom said, when she left

"She's got a cheek," Iris said. "She's lucky she's not a murderess."

"I think she should be given a chance," Clair said. "If Richard and the rest of the investors get their money back, then that's a good thing, isn't it."

"I'm inclined to agree with Clair. I think he'd like to keep quiet about the stolen money." Tom said.

"Up to you two. I'm washing my hands of it." Iris didn't hide her annoyance, she stood up and left the room.

A minute later Mandy returned carrying a laptop in a shoulder bag in one hand and a briefcase in the other. She put them both on the kitchen table and sat down, opened the case and took some documents out, handing them to Tom.

He took the laptop out of the bag and signed on and using the information provided by Mandy he logged on to Ken Birkenshaw's offshore account. The money was still intact and Mandy had given him the authority to access it.

"Where's the account number and passwords where the money came from, Mandy?"

"Are you going to keep quiet about my involvement?"

"I will say that I don't remember anything of the evening prior to the accident. Which is partly true. I will not mention coming to your flat. That's all I'm prepared to do."

"And if I deny you were at my place, you'll not contradict me?"

"I've already said. It is covered by me saying I don't remember anything of that evening."

"No I mean you ever coming to my flat?"

"Don't be stupid, Mandy. That's an unnecessary lie and I'll not lie to the police for you. We had a relationship and you mentioned to Ken that I looked like his identical twin. Just leave it at that."

Clair observed how Tom handled the situation and was pleased he didn't allow Mandy to have all her own way. But she couldn't help a twinge of jealousy brushing her heart.

Mandy screwed up her face thinking about Tom's advice. "Ok. I agree." She dug into the briefcase and handed him the rest of the paperwork to access the Development Property Account.

It took under two minutes for Tom to transfer the money back to where it belonged.

"Right," he said to Clair, "Time for you to ring Richard and tell him the money is back in his account and if he wants to know how then he'll have to visit in person, either here or at your place."

"Let's get some facts straight before I ring." Clair turned to Mandy. "You are happy if we don't mention that you brought the necessary paperwork to us?"

"Yes. I don't want Richard to know I had anything to do with Ken's theft or helping you to get it returned." Mandy said. Then she held up the briefcase. "This is Ken's. It's where he kept all those documents. Can't you say he brought it with him?"

"Well, that's true." Clair said, looking at Tom for confirmation.

Tom nodded. "Fine with me." then he looked through the briefcase and found his debit card in one of the small pockets. He glanced at it then put it in his back pocket. Mandy had watched but thought it wise to keep quiet..

Clair used Iris's landline to ring Richard and she briefly explained to him the events of the previous night and mentioned they were to be interviewed by the police the following day.. He was shocked Ken had died but recovered admirably when she told him the money had been returned and advised he checked the account. He asked for more details. Clair said it was a complicated story and suggested he visit and she would give him all the information she had.

"Could I see you this afternoon, say about two thirty?" he said, obviously anxious to know what they were going to say to the police.

"We are at Iris's. Do you know the address?"

"Yes, and thank you, Clair." he said and rang off.

"All done." Clair said.

Mandy stood, saying, "I think I need to freshen up."

They watched her leave the room.

"That woman is a scheming, tart, Tom. I'm surprised you got involved with her."

Tom shrugged. "You know what men are like when they've had a few drinks, sweetheart."

"Well you'd better have more control in future."

Tom smiled. Clair was more or less saying they had a future together. He got up and kissed her on the lips. "Anything for you, gorgeous," he said, when they parted.

CHAPTER 23

Richard arrived at two-thirty and Iris showed him into the sitting-room where Clair and Tom were waiting. When he saw Tom, he stopped in the doorway his lips curling in anger, and said, "Ken?" He then looked at Clair, his anger etching his face. "If this is some sort of joke, I don't think it funny, Clair. You told me he was killed yesterday."

Clair put her hand on Tom's arm. "This is Tom Armstrong and not my husband, Ken Birkenshaw. I suggest you sit down and let us tell you what happened."

Richard looked from Clair to Tom and then Iris. "Iris? Is she right?"

"Yes, Richard, and I suggest you take a seat. She motioned him to one of the settees and asked if he would like any refreshments.

Richard sat and said, "Just some tonic water, if you don't mind."

Mandy, who had been out of the room when Richard arrived, entered, and sat in one of the chairs. Tom noticed she had increased her limp.

Richard looked surprised to see her. "What are you doing here, Mandy? I had a message to say you were ill."

"Ken forced me to come. He had this revolver, Richard." Mandy paused, and a look passed between her and Richard that caused him to thin his lips and turn his eyes cold. Mandy continued. "He intended to shoot me."

"Why? I thought you and he were close friends."

"We were, but then he changed….I think you'd better hear what Clair has to say. It will explain a lot."

Clair was sitting with Tom on the settee opposite Richard. He looked at Clair and raised an eyebrow.

"As I said, Richard. Tom is not my husband and Ken did die last night. He actually shot himself accidentally. Tom as you can see is identical to Ken. But very different in character. Tom is the one who transferred the money back to your account. You have checked it?"

"The money is back where it belongs," Richard said, staring at Tom. "Are you the person I spoke to when I visited Clair?"

Tom smiled. "That's me, Mr Cartwright. But I had lost my memory and Clair and Dr Miller at the hospital assumed I was Ken Birkenshaw because of our likeness to each other. Very confusing for me and very confusing for Clair when I acted differently to her husband."

"And how did you recover my firm's money?"

Tom reached down by the arm of the settee and brought up the briefcase. "With the documents in here," he said, and handed it across to Cartwright.

Richard opened the case and brought out some of the paperwork. A quick glance showed him they contained passwords and codes to an off-shore bank. He pushed the paperwork back inside the briefcase, closed the catch and put it on the floor beside his leg.

"Thank you for being so honest, Tom. And don't call me Mr Cartwright. After what you did, I'm thanking my lucky stars. Call me Richard and bring me up to date."

Clair let Tom do the explaining because he had lived the nightmare and actually suffered far more than her.

When Tom finished explaining the events leading up to Ken Birkenshaw's death, Richard said, "So you are a computer programmer, Tom. You wouldn't like to come and work for me, would you? I could do with someone to beef up my computer security."

Tom smiled. "Not my speciality, I'm afraid, Richard. And I'm self employed."

Richard turned to Clair. "Coming back to your husband, Clair. I knew he was a bit of a rogue and he could sell eggs to a batch of hens, but from what you say, he was a crackpot."

"He was a psychopath. No two ways about it," Iris said. She had been refreshing drinks during Richard's illumination of events.

"I understand you are all going to be interviewed by the police tomorrow. What do you intend to tell them about Ken Birkenshaw stealing my firm's money?" Richard said, looking at Clair and Tom sitting opposite.

"That's up to you, Richard." Tom said.

"Well, I don't want the theft or the return of the money to become general knowledge. As you know I asked for it to be returned by Tuesday. That has happened, and I would like to keep quiet about it."

"The police will want a motive for Ken wanting to kill us all last night." Clair said. "We know why he wanted to kill Iris and Mandy, they knew about him and Tom being identical and his plan to steal Tom's identity. But the police will want to know why he was after Tom's identity and was prepared to kill Tom for it."

"Um, sticky wicket." Richard mused.

"Why can't you be honest with the police and

ask them to keep quiet about the theft." Iris said.

"It doesn't work that way, Iris. The police are duty bound to investigate the fraud once they know about it. And there are reporters who have sources in our law community. Too much of a risk of investors finding out and it could mean a loss of trust in the firm. The exodus could bankrupt me and the company."

"Ah, the me, me, me syndrome" Iris said, with a sneer.

"No! Not just me!" Richard turned on her angrily. "There are several property developments in progress, and over a thousand construction workers who will lose their jobs if my firm is bankrupted."

Tom could see Iris taking a breath to continue the argument. "Can we just leave that aside for the moment and concentrate on finding a solution," he said.

"To hell with it." Iris said, giving Richard her blackest look.

"Please, Iris," Clair said. "Tom is right. And we need your expertise as an accountant."

"All. right. I would advise sailing close to honesty as the best bet. The police are not stupid."

"Thank you, Iris." Richard said. "And I agree an outright lie would not work with expert investigators."

Tom had been thinking. The money was back where it belonged. The police need not know it had been stolen. "What if Ken was planning to steal the money, rather than actually stolen it?"

"Tom Armstrong, you are worth a million dollars!" Richard said, smiling broadly. "Simple solution, sailing close to honesty Everyone agree?"

"What if they found out the money went then came back?" Clair asked.

"Oh, it would be difficult to prove," Richard said, still smiling. "I'll show them the offshore account contract in Ken's name but not the transactions. It will be proof enough that he was planning something. and offshore banks are notorious for not assisting law enforcement. It's their livelihood to keep their customers transactions private. And I've just had another thought. I will leak a rumour saying Ken was planning a theft of company funds. But our security system stopped him doing it."

"You are as devious as Ken Birkenshaw," Iris said.

Clair was worried her basic honesty would stop her from telling lies to the police. "I don't like the thought of lying."

"No need to lie, Clair," Richard said. "Officially you don't know anything about the theft. All you have to say is I came to see you today and when I was here Tom gave me Ken's brief case. When I opened it I found out Ken had been planning to steal money from the firm."

Tom could see Clair was still worried. "Could you tell us what Ken was planning to do, Richard?"

Richard stared at Tom, and Tom stared back at Richard with a bland look on his face. Richard realised what Tom was implying.

"Clair, listen to me. I found out your husband was planning to steal money from our firm when Tom gave me a briefcase your husband had brought with him last night. Do you understand? Or do you want me to repeat it."

Clair stared at Richard, a puzzled frown on her face for a few seconds, but then understood. "I understand, perfectly, Richard. You told me Ken had planned to steal money from the firm and you found out when Tom gave you his case. All true."

"Just stick with that, Clair and you won't be lying."

Richard picked up the briefcase, stood up and, gave Clair a peck on the cheek. `He tried to do the same to Iris but she backed away. Her face was emotionless. Richard turned to Tom and held out his hand for Tom to shake, "If you ever want a job, Tom, get in touch."

Richard turned to Mandy who had also stood. "When can I expect you back at work, Mandy," His tone was cool, his face unsmiling.

Mandy guessed he wasn't completely fooled by her not being involved in Ken Birkenshaw's plans.

"Could you give me a week, Richard? I injured my knee helping Tom to disarm Ken, and the police want to interview me again. I assume they will ask if I knew where Ken got the gun from."

Richard stared at Mandy assessing what she had said. "A week, then. I'll see you next Monday."

Iris showed him out.

Tom stared at Mandy. She, knowing what he was thinking, smiled back at him. "Well, it was my body that hit him off balance, Tom.

Clair rolled her eyes.

Tom and Clair were pleased when Mandy Sitwell decided to return to her flat shortly after Cartwright left.

CHAPTER 24

The interview with Inspector Jones and Sergeant Blakeley took place in Iris's dining room. It consisted of him going over their statements of the night Ken Berkenshaw accidentally killed himself to clear up the issue of the gun.

"Could you tell me where your husband acquired the gun, Mrs Birkenshaw?"

"No, sorry Inspector, I didn't even know Ken owned a gun."

"Well we traced it to the MOD from the serial number, but they couldn't help us further. I have already spoken to Miss Sitwell. She said she'd never seen it before, either. Same with Richard Cartwright, who I understand was a close friend of the deceased. The problem we have is we can't trace where the gun came from. There was only your husband's prints and a few smudges on it.

He then interviewed Tom and Clair to hear their account of the events which were Birkenshaw's motive to murder four people.

Clair provided photographs of her husband on their wedding day and a video which was made of the wedding ceremony. Inspector Jones was fascinated by the identical likeness of Tom Armstrong and Ken Birkenshaw. He was of the same opinion as Iris King, there was a family connection. The fingerprints and the DNA submitted on the night Birkenshaw died did not match the two men. But the DNA had many similarities supporting the theory the two men were connected by blood ties. Tom decided it was time to speak to his aunt Alice in the hope she could clarify if he was an identical twin.

During the interview Inspector Jones wanted to know if Mandy Sitwell was in any way involved in the attempted murder of Tom. Tom stuck to the story he'd already agreed with Mandy. He could not remember anything from the time he left his flat on that Friday evening to when he recovered consciousness the following Wednesday. He also explained it was not until Birkenshaw tried to run him down he recovered his memory and recalled his identity. It was obvious from the Inspector's attitude he was unconvinced with Tom's answer but had to accept it. He had Sergeant Blakeley make a note to contact Dr Miller.

It was the same when it came to the amount of money Birkenshaw was planning to steal. Tom said Richard Cartwright could be the one to answer that question. When Jones put the question to Clair she said, knowing her husband, it was probably millions. She was glad when he didn't press the issue or see how tightly she clasped her hands together under the table.

The next day Tom had a call from Dr Miller. He'd heard the news on the local radio about the death of Ken Birkenshaw. He asked if Tom could visit him at the hospital for the record of his name and personal details to be amended. He would also like to examine him in light of the new facts. Tom agreed and they made an appointment for the following day.

The medical examination carried out by Dr Miller was more of him listening to how Tom was almost murdered rather than a medical update. He took copious notes, some to correct Tom's personal details held by the hospital, others for personal use. He mentioned to Tom he might use the case to submit a paper on aspects of brain trauma, assuring Tom no names would be included. Finally, he gave Tom a brief examination and declared him to be in good health.

When Tom arrived back at Clair's he was besieged by newspaper reporters and several TV crews who were jostling for his attention when he stepped out of the taxi. They were like rowdy school children, shouting questions and creating a hullabaloo that was deafening: "Are you Tom Armstrong? "Was Birkenshaw your brother?" "How much did he try to steal?" "Did you kill him?", were only a few Tom could make out. He put his head down and using his size and weight pushed through the melee to get to the gates which were shut, A six-foot-six man, in a black security uniform, stood behind it His face remained impassive but he opened the gate enough for Tom to squeeze through.

"Thank's," Tom said. "Who are you?"

"Security, sir. Mrs Birkenshaw called my boss when these hooligans turned up."

Clair opened the front door and as soon as Tom entered the house, she said, "I tried to ring you, Tom. And I've left dozens of messages, warning you there was a pack of media wolves at our gate. Did you turn your phone off?"

Tom took his new mobile out of his pocket and switched it on. "I had to turn it off at the hospital. Sorry, sweetheart, I forgot to switch it back on."

"Iris has a similar rabble at her house as well. She rang to say she's packing a bag and going to stay with some friends until the hounds have another prey to chase."

"You think we should do the same?" Tom asked, looking through the leaded hall window.

"It would make sense."

"May be a good time for us to go to my place in London. I'm going to have to collect my things when I move here. We could spend a few days there at least."

"I'll pack a few things." Clair said, moving towards the stairs.

"I'll book a taxi to get us to the station." Tom said, starting to dial.

Clair stopped and said, "No need, darling. Rolf will be able to take us when we leave."

"Rolf?"

"Big boy at the gate. He works for Enfield Security, a firm Ken used to employ. I know Frank Enfield well and he supplied Rolf at short notice, but explained he can only be here a few hours. His car is round the back. When we are ready, I'll buzz him."

"The more I know you, sweetheart, the more you amaze me." and he walked over to her and kissed her firmly on the lips.

The train pulled away from Sheffield in drizzling rain and arrived at St Pancras in weak sunshine. Tom and Clair used a black cab to take them to Chiswick.

Clair wasn't impressed by Tom's flat, a small sitting room furnished with a couch, a long table carrying a desktop computer attached to a 27" monitor, two laptops surround by a number electronic gadgets, comfortable looking swivel chair, pushed under the table, and a bare wood floor. A galley kitchen could be seen through an archway, and a bedroom through an open door opposite. Clair walked over to the bedroom and was not pleased with the single bed, nor the en suite with a shower one could hardly turn round in.

Tom smiled at her grimace.

"Do you want to freshen up first, love," he grinned. "Or shall we use the shower together?"

"You must be joking, Tom Armstrong. "I'll be lucky to fit in there by myself. Me first."

"Dress smart, I'll' be taking you out for an evening meal," he said, carrying in their luggage and dumping the two cases on the bed.

Clair could have sworn the bed creaked in protest and wondered how on earth they would both be able to sleep in it. She chose a lilac knee length dress to wear and she let the natural wave in her hair fall loose to her shoulders. Tom thought she looked stunning. He had dressed in a white shirt with a subdued blue tie. His blonde hair was now the length of a brush cut. Clair thought he was the most handsome loveable man she'd ever met. He rarely reminded her of her deceased husband. They may have looked alike but Tom's caring character and genuine love for her wiped Ken Birkenshaw from her mind most of the time.

The restaurant Tom took her to had a small dining room with defused lighting, soft unobtrusive music, and floor length windows overlooking the Thames, the black water reflecting the myriad lights from the city buildings. All the other tables were full and each table had an arrangement of four chairs, but most only had two diners of various ages.

They both had lobster, the house wine but no desert. When they were finished Clair leaned back in her chair and blew out her cheeks.

"Wew," she said. One thing about you, Tom Armstrong, you know how to treat a lady. Romantic restaurant, great food and expensive wine. Anyone would think you were trying to woo me into bed."

"Didn't I tell you, young Clair, I've given it up for Lent."

"Lent? That finished last week."

"Oh, good." They grinned across the small dining table at each other.

Clair thinking, I'll probably have to sleep on top.

When Clair used the loo, Tom paid the bill and ordered a taxi to take them to Chiswick. The journey wasn't long but they used the time in the back of the taxi to have a romantic cuddle, the street lamps flickering on their faces. The taxi pulled into the driveway of a large mock Tudor house.

Clair and Tom stood together until the taxi drove off, Clair running her eyes over the building and looking bemused. Tom, gazed at her, a quiet smile on his lips.

"Where are we? Where's your flat?"

Tom walked over to an ornamental urn placed by the side of the door, lifted a corner and brought out a key and as he used it to open the front door, he said," "Come on, young lady, this is where we are staying for the week."

Clair followed him, a thousand questions hammering to get out. She was struck silent by the opulence of her surroundings when Tom pressed a switch to turn on the lights. Seeing her wide open eyes darting over the dark, expensive antique furniture and the great beams reaching across the ceiling above them, he smiled and was pleased he'd decided to bring her here rather than his grim little flat.

She turned to him, finally finding her voice. "How?"

"A friend who is away, working in America for a month or two. He lets me use it, provided I keep an eye on the place."

"He must be rich."

"All my friends are rich, sweetheart. But not all with money. Let's take a tour, then to bed."

"What about nightclothes? Mine are at your flat?"

Tom grinned at her "The bedrooms have underfloor heating, love. I'm sure you'll manage somehow."

For the rest of the week they used the Tudor mansion as their base and Tom organised visits to the main tourist attractions. The first day, Tom booked a visit to the Eye and Clair was thrilled. She had always wanted to ride in one of those pods, but somehow never had. She kept moving around the pod, trying to see every aspect of London as the wheel turned on its axis. Tom thought, for a woman of twenty-five Clair sometimes showed the wonder and the sheer innocent happiness of a teenager. It didn't take a genius to see why she had been unsuitable for Ken Birkenshaw.

And as the days skipped along, Tom and Clair's relationship blossomed into a deep loving friendship and they found in each other a soulmate, a term often written about in romantic fiction but rarely found in real life. They decided to marry, Tom didn't actually propose but it came up in their conversation on the last evening in London. They were strolling along the Thames embankment planning how Tom could work from Clair's house. She said he could use Ken's old office for his computer work, if it was big enough. And she offered to teach him to drive, saying, "You'll need a car when you live in my part of the country, darling. You just can't stick your arm in the air and shout "Taxi". And if you want to walk to Sheffield for a nine o'clock meeting you'll have to set off at 5 am."

"So when do you want to get married, sweetheart?"

"Could you give me six months, darling. It's a decent time, don't you think? And I would like an old fashioned engagement period. What about a Christmas wedding?"

"Christmas sounds great," Tom said, and pulled Clair towards him, "Damn, I forgot to propose. Right, I'll need to buy an engagement ring. And a morning suit and a top hat."

"I'm pleased you agree, Tom Armstrong. Oh, forget the formal gear. A lounge suit will do just fine." And they kissed,

CHAPTER 25

When they arrived back at the old farmhouse they were relieved to find it free of the media hoard. They had avoided watching any TV or listening to any news channels while the were enjoying the visit to London.

Clair and Iris had been in touch during the week and Clair knew her sister had arrived home the previous day. Clair gave her a ring.

After a brief conversation Iris said, "There's been quite a news coverage of Ken Birkenshaw while we were away. I forgot to cancel the news-papers and I've browsed them. The first few days we were away he was front page news. But as the week progressed he faded to the inside pages and then dropped all together."

"Good! The less I hear about Ken, the hap-pier I'll be." Clair said. "I have a letter from the pathologist to say his body has been released to the undertakers. And I have a letter from them asking me to get in touch."

Iris ignored the fact Clair had once been been so in love with that bastard she had seen no wrong in him. Her sister deserved to be shot of him and lucky she had found a healthier love with Tom Armstrong. "I understand. But you might be interested to hear about his mother and step-father. His mother had been married to a rather wealthy man before he gambled away his money and committed suicide. She then married a drug dealer and became a druggie herself. They both died of an overdose when Birkenshaw was twelve. One report said he was abused by his stepfather for years. When his parents died he went from one care home to another."

"Maybe that's what turned him into a criminal," Clair said.

"No, Clair. Except for the abuse, Tom had a similar upbringing and look at him."

"You're right. What about the birth certificate. Does it show a link between Tom and Ken?"

"No, it doesn't and that has flummoxed me. He was born in Sheffield and a month or so after Tom. Doesn't make sense to me."

"I'll have a word with Tom and see what he has to say. Thanks for letting me know."

"Iris is right," Tom said when Clair told him. "It doesn't make sense. My DNA was a close match to Ken Birkenshaw and I think there is a good chance he was my twin brother. I've already decided I want to have a word with my aunt Alice. If anyone knows the truth, it will be her."

Tom had not receive telephone calls because

his mobile had been destroyed but when he set up his new computer there were forty odd emails from friends and acquaintances wanting to know if he was alright. He sent a BCC email, to the majority writing he and Clair were fine and thanking them for their interest and adding his new mobile number. But to a few he either rang or sent a specific email outlining in more detail the events leading up to Birkenshaw's death.

One of these emails he sent to Garry Willman in America, entrepreneur, longtime friend and the one who let him use the house in Chiswick, thanking him for the loan of the house and letting him know that during his stay he had proposed to Clair and they were planning a Christmas wedding. Would he like to come?

"Try stopping me, Blondie! And I thought you said you had no intention of marrying until you were sixty-five and only then to get a free housekeeper."

Tom replied, "Hadn't met the girl of my dreams then, G. See you at the wedding."

Jeff had sent him an email, not only asking if he was ok, but also saying the initial sales of the KINSMAN were very promising, and he had been trying to contact him on the phone for several days. Tom rang, explained about the mobile and they made arrangements to have a meal together so Tom could bring him up to date. Jeff volunteered to book the meal and suggested they make it a foursome by inviting Emma and Clair along. "Oh, you don't mind lunch rather than an evening meal, do you, Tom? It's just that it would be more convenient for us because Kim will be in school."

Tom had a quick conversation with Clair and they agreed.

Jeff rang back later to say lunch was booked for one o'clock and if they came to his house they could walk to the restaurant from there and save the trouble of finding a parking place.

Tom agreed but had a sinking feeling in his stomach and hoped he would be able to eat his lunch tomorrow.

When Tom introduced Clair to Emma and Jeff, Tom was surprised how much Clair and Emma looked alike. They were almost the same height, both slim and had dark hair and brown eyes. They were both wearing similar dresses, high neck and knee length, Clair's pink, Emma's blue. Both were elegant and beautiful. Extraordinary. Nobody else commented on the similarity. So he decided to keep quiet.

They set off for the restaurant and Tom knew even before they turned the final corner and saw the restaurant in front of them he had guessed right the previous day. It was the same place where Mandy had mistaken him for Ken Birkenshaw. He just hoped today was not going to lead to attempted murder and the death of a psychopath.

Ken Birkenshaw was cremated.   Clair arranged a simple service at the crematorium without the eulogy. The mourners were sparse. Clair, Tom, Iris and her parents as the family mourners. To be accurate Clair was the only family mourner. Her parents and Tom were there to support her, Iris to see the bastard was finally off this earth. Four friends from his business contacts turned up but no one attended from Richard Cartwright's firm. Not even Mandy Sitwell appeared. Three female friends of Clair attended and hugged her when the service was over.

Two strangers were also at the service. Both in their mid forties, both looking fit, their faces tanned from long periods outdoors, and both dressed in suits with white shirts and black ties. They sat at the back of the crematorium and after the service, Tom approached them to find out if his guess of who they were was right. "Excuse me, folks," He said, "You wouldn't happened to be my Archangels by any chance?"

"Pardon?" The taller of the two," said, giving Tom a puzzled stare.

"Well, I was told that if two hikers hadn't come along when they did, and took care of me until the paramedics arrived, my chances of surviving the crash at the Snake would have been zero. I'm guessing you were those men. Am I right?"

Dave turned to his mate. "He's not only a miracle man, Mick. He's a flaming brilliant detective as well." He turned back to Tom with a smile and held out his hand to shake. "My name is Dave Hanson and this is Mick Botham. Yes, and we are the hikers you were told about."

Tom shook hands with both men and said, "It's Tom, and I'm really pleased to meet you both. Come and meet meet my fiancé, Clair and her family."

"Oh, we couldn't do that, Tom," Dave said. "We just wanted to see for ourselves that you had recovered. And maybe tell you how thankful we are that things turned out ok for you."

"Just hang on a minute, please." Tom saw that Clair's friends were leaving and Clair was walking back to where her parents and Iris were talking to Ken's friends. He waved her over and then introduced her to Dave and Mick. "These are my two Archangels, sweetheart. Remember we were told how lucky I was that they were at the crash site?"

"I didn't do anything." Mick said, before Clair had a chance to say anything. "It was Dave, here, who looked after you. Used his coat to keep you warm and his emergency kit to bandage your head."

Dave glared at Mick. "Shut up, Mick. We were a team."

Clair held out her hand to shake with both of them, and said, "We will be forever in your debt, both of you." She turned to Tom. "We should do something as a thank you, don't you think, sweetheart?"

Tom nodded. "You are regular hikers, I understand?"

"Oh, no. We don't want anything." Dave turned to Mick. "Do we, mate?"

Mick shook his head emphatically. "No, Tom. Honestly, we are just glad you are alive and well."

"Come on, Mick," Dave said, and started to walk away.

"Well, could you leave a contact number, phone or email. And would you be in favour of me and Clair taking you out for a meal or something? It's the least we could do."

"A pint will do fine," Dave said. "You ok with that?"

"Fine, Dave." Tom said, and gave Clair's elbow a gentle squeeze to stop her protesting. "Phone numbers and I'll be in touch."

Dave and Mick submitted their mobile numbers and they all shook hands again before Dave and Mick walked off.

Clair turned to Tom with steel in her eyes. "A pint, Tom Armstrong. How can you be so mean?"

"Ah, Clair, my beautiful, innocent little chicken. When I turn up for that pint, I will hand them a present each that you and I will bicker over for the next few days. I was thinking of a top of the range smart phone each. With GPS and a range of local walking maps."

"I might have guessed it would be blinking computers. I shall have to put my thinking cap on."

They walked back to join the rest of the party.

There was no wake or reception. Clair was of the opinion Ken had received a proper send off at the crematorium and a group of people drinking and eating to his memory would have been a farce.

At least she had part closure, there was still the coroner's inquest to come.

Clair's parents, John and Anne King, had arrived the day before Ken's funeral and had arranged to stay with Iris. She organised an evening dinner and Tom was formally introduced to them when he and Clair turned up for the meal. They had already spoken to him via FaceTime and had come to accept him as Clair's fiancé. Clair's mother had no qualms about him becoming one of the family after Clair described how he had saved her, not once but twice from her murderous husband. Clair's father was more cautious, having been completely fooled by Birkenshaw. He quizzed Tom when they sat in Iris's summer house, sipping their respective beer.

John King gave Tom a penetrating stare and sighed. "I know I shouldn't be biased against you, Tom, but you are the spitting image of that bastard, Birkenshaw. And every time I see you with Clair I think what a fool I was to believe she was lucky to have such a charming and industrious husband."

"I don't think for a minute you were a fool, John. He convinced his friends, neighbours and he even convinced Clair he was a normal human being. Iris and Richard Cartwright are the only two I've met who were not fooled by him.

"Yes. but I was a solicitor, it was my job to assess clients and separate the rogues from the victims."

"Oh, I think if you had him as a client you would not have been fooled for long. I understand from what Clair has told me you only occasionally spent time in his company. And don't forget he was brilliant at playing the part of man about town, charming, courteous and friendly. And I think, going bankrupt and trying to keep it a secret was stressing him to breaking point."

"You may be right, Tom. And listening to you trying to make it easier for me to stop kicking myself over Ken Birkenshaw has made me realise how different you are from him. And if Clair can fall in love with you despite looking exactly like him I'll do my best not to keep comparing you to him."

"Thank you."

John King sighed again, and in a jokey sombre voice, said, "Now young Tom. As a potential husband of my youngest daughter, it is my duty to ask what your future prospects are?"

Tom matched the tone. "I'm a down and out computer programmer Mr King, who has recently been informed his video KINSMAN is about to make him a millionaire."

"Oh, good. As a down and out ex solicitor who can't afford to pay his bills, I expect a hand out when I come calling." He held out his hand and they shook firmly.

CHAPTER 26

Tom wanted a face to face meeting with his aunt to talk about what could be a sensitive subject to her. He guessed there must be a good reason for her not to tell him if he had a twin brother. He rang his aunt and asked if he could visit with his fiancé and her sister. His aunt said of course. When he offered Iris the chance to hear what his aunt had to say, she thumped him on the arm. "Do you want to put a bet on it?" Tom just shook his head and smiled. Even he believe it was possible after the results of the DNA tests.

Alice knew why he wanted to see her. She had heard on the radio and read in the newspaper how Ken Birkenshaw had tried to murder Tom. And Tom had already contacted her via email the day after Birkenshaw had died to assure her he was unharmed and to warn her she would probably hear some lurid accounts of what had taken place. Tom was her only nephew but they had never been close. She was an independent woman and while she could relate to her pupils and had been an excellent teacher, she had no wish to have children of her own. She did regret she hadn't done more to support Tom when he was growing up. For an educated woman, she thought, what a fool she had been.

She lived in a three bedroom detached bungalow in the village of Warmthorpe, roughly 15 miles from Nottingham. The village had a corner shop clinging to existence by giving excellent service to the village and surrounding community. The pub thrived by serving locally sourced ingredients at a reasonable price and cooked by a Michelin three star chef. She had retired from teaching the previous year and since then immersed herself in the village social life - from arts and crafts to teaching privately youngsters who were struggling at school. She had become plump in recent years but kept fit by walking the country trails around the village. Alice's hair had gone grey early and she had it set every week by the local hairdresser to keep it neat. Her face could look friendly and kind for social intercourse or authoritative and stern for children who needed discipline.

Alice welcomed them at her front door by giving Tom a peck on the cheek and doing the same with Clair and Iris when he introduced them. She then said, "Come on through, it's far too nice an afternoon to be indoors,"

They followed her through to the patio, where a set of outdoor cane chairs had been placed around a matching table. A jug of home made lemonade and four glasses sat on a metal tray in the middle of the table. The patio overlooked a small garden enclosed by a six foot wooden fence, Raised flower beds filled with a variety of winter pansies and polyanthus gave a marvellous show of purple, yellow, pink and white flowers. The warm sunshine was unusual for early May and the patio, sheltered from a frisky breeze, was the ideal place to chat outdoors. Alice offered round the lemonade, saying, "Home made, and delicious, if I say so myself. My latest fad."

They could hardly refuse after that introduction.

"Now then, Tom, I've been hearing news you've had an adventurous time. Surviving a murder plot and helping to put an end to the murderer. And even more thrilling, falling in love with this beautiful young lady."

Clair blushed an adorable pink.

Tom laughed at Aunt Alice's literary description. She had taught english lit. to budding teenagers. "Yes, falling in love with Clair, and she agreeing to marry me was well worth all the hassle that went before."

"Will you two stop it," Clair said, "You are embarrassing me. And it's rude to talk about somebody when they are present."

"Too true, young lady," Alice said. "You should be ashamed of yourself, Tom."

They all laughed. Tom raised his glass, "To my favourite Aunt." And sipped some lemonade. They all followed his example. "Hey up, Aunt, this is really refreshing." Clair and Iris agreed.

Iris, who was anxious to find out if Tom and Ken Birkenshaw were from the same egg, said with her usual forthright tone, "I don't know about those two lovebirds, but I came to see you, Alice, to find out if I'm right and that Tom and Ken Berkenshaw were twins?"

Alice frowned at Iris. "Why?" There was a school mistress authority in that one word.

Iris was unabashed. "Curiosity, I suppose. And a mystery I would love solved."

Alice stared hard at Iris, then her face softened. "'Curiosity', was a trait I encouraged in my students. It is one of the important building blocks to human development. But what I'm going to reveal to Tom is for his ears only. If he wishes to share the information with you and Clair, it will be up to him."

Iris looked disappointed. But Clair stood up straight away, smiled at Tom, turned to her sister and said, "Come on, nosy, you'll get to know eventually."

"I've prepared coffee and snacks, they are in the kitchen. It's to the left of the front door. Help yourselves," Alice said, and watched as they entered the bungalow.

She looked across at Tom who was sitting next to her, a hand on the table. She reached across and laid her hand on top of his. "I'm sorry, Tom, but there is a strong reason why I kept quiet about what happened to your brother. Despite the reason, I think it was wrong you were not told you had a twin when you were old enough to deal with it. It is entirely my fault."

Tom gazed at her and saw there were tears forming in the corners of her eyes. He turned his hand over and squeezed her hand sympathetically. "I wouldn't blame you, Aunt. Knowing you, I know you thought you were doing right at the time."

Alice released her hand from his and took out a lace handkerchief to dab at her eyes. "No, Tom, I never thought it was right. It was to keep my promise to your mother."

"And the promise was?"

"To keep quiet your mother and father sold your brother to a criminal midwife for ten thousand pounds."

"My god, why?"

"Your father had the chance to buy into the engineering firm he worked for."

"And my mother went along with it?"

"It was she who encouraged him. She told me she was fed up scraping from month to month. And two sons would be too much of a sacrifice. She wanted her life back."

"Were they poor, then? My mother and father?"

'No, I wouldn't say poor. But she'd had a good job before marrying your father, and while he was a good engineer he'd been made redundant from his previous firm shortly after he married my sister. They had to give up their house because they couldn't pay the mortgage. Your grandparents were not in a financial position to help them."

"But selling a baby, Aunt! From what I remember of them they were always kind and loving. I couldn't have had a happier childhood until they were killed."

"Yes, I know, Tom. And if it is any comfort to you, Marion regretted it later. And she told me often she wished she could go back in time to undo what even she came to regard as an evil act."

"So what happened to my twin."

"He was sold on to another couple. I tried to find out who but the midwife refused to part with any details. Your mother wanted to hire a private investigator to find the couple, but your father pointed out, if he knew why he was investigating he could blackmail them for the rest of their lives."

"So you didn't know what had happened to my brother until he tried to kill me?"

"Yes, and that's why I regret more than ever not telling you about him. If you and he had known it may have stopped him attempting to murder you."

"Oh, I don't think so, Aunt. It's like Iris said, he proved to be a psychopath in the end."

They both sat there for a minute or so, thinking their respective thoughts. Then Tom said, "Why didn't Grandad and Grandma want to look after me when Mum and Dad died?"

"Because they found out you mother had sold your brother. Marion, your mum, had just told me and we were arguing over what she had done, just after you were born. We must have started shouting at each other and Mum walked in on us, wanting to know what all the fuss was about. Marion blurted out the story, not thinking how it would affect Mum. She went white and slapped Marion so hard she nearly fell off the chair she was sitting on. And don't forget, your mother was still recovering from having twins."

"Grandma must have been in shock, Aunt. Can't help feeling sorry for both of them. So what happened next?"

"Your grandmother and grandfather were religious, When we were children they insisted we went to church with them every Sunday. Well, by this time Marion was sobbing with pain and a bucket full of different emotions, and I tried to reason with Mum. Mentioning, Marion was still recovering from giving birth to twins. It was as if I'd lit a match in a gas filled room. Mum exploded with righteous anger, calling us wicked and wonton sluts and then ordered Marion and me to pack our bags and get out of her house."

"But why you?"

"Oh, I was tarred with the same brush, Tom. Both me and Marion had stopped going to church when we reached our mid teens and Mum was always getting on at Dad to discipline us. Poor Dad. Having two daughters and a wife to contend with drove him to an early grave, I think." Alice smiled at Tom showing she was only joking. "And Mum never wanted to see either of us from then on. And you suffered the sins of your parents, I'm afraid, Tom."

"Lucky I had Granddad, Will, then. Did you know he came to the school when I was sixteen and asked if I'd like to live with him. I accepted his offer like a shot. And he was great to me. Helping with my homework and I think if it wasn't for him, I'd never have gone to Uni. He wasn't just a granddad but a friend as well. It really broke me up when he died two years ago."

"Ah, yes he was a lovely gent. Always cheerful despite his constant ill health." Alice gazed at Tom with sympathetic eyes, before asking, "So what are you going to do now you know Ken Birkenshaw was your twin brother?"

"Well, I know most of the history of Ken from the media. I don't want to know about him any more. And I think Clair and Iris will say the same."

On the way back home, Iris drove and Clair sat in the back with Tom to hear what Alice had told him. They were both shocked to hear his mother had sold his twin brother to the midwife. And the only thing to please Iris was that she had been proved right Ken and Tom were identical twins.

"My aunt is concerned about what you might do now you know," Tom said.

"Well, I'll not say anything, Tom," Clair said, and kissed him on the lips. "There, my lips are sealed."

"Iris?" Tom said.

"For my sister's sake and yours, Tom, I have no intention to broadcast it."

"Thank you both. You really are lovely ladies. How about I take you both out for a decent meal this evening. You two chose where."

Clair and Iris debated which was the best restaurant in Sheffield all the way home.

THE END

Printed in Great Britain
by Amazon

78326643R00139